DAY
OF THE
DEAD

A

DAY OF THE DEAD

A WYNN CABOT MYSTERY

DREW GOLDEN

First published by Level Best Books 2022

Copyright © 2022 by Drew Golden

All rights reserved. No part of this publication may be reproduced, stored or transmitted in any form or by any means, electronic, mechanical, photocopying, recording, scanning, or otherwise without written permission from the publisher. It is illegal to copy this book, post it to a website, or distribute it by any other means without permission.

This novel is entirely a work of fiction. The names, characters and incidents portrayed in it are the work of the author's imagination. Any resemblance to actual persons, living or dead, events or localities is entirely coincidental.

Drew Golden asserts the moral right to be identified as the author of this work.

First edition

ISBN: 978-1-68512-202-7

Cover art by Level Best Designs

This book was professionally typeset on Reedsy. Find out more at reedsy.com

Praise for the Wayne Cabot Mysteries

Praise for *Nouveau Noir*

Greed and grapes lead to murder in this clever tale.—*Kirkus Reviews*

Nouveau Noir is an intricate murder mystery anchored by its charming rookie agent and colorful cast.—*Foreword* Clarion Reviews

Readers will enjoy the engaging characters in *Nouveau Noir*.—Blue Ink Review

Drew Golden took care in every aspect of this novel, and the result is a fantastic story worthy of 4 out of 4 stars. I would recommend it to anyone who enjoys a good crime novel, especially one comprising layers of intrigue. I would look forward to reading any additional books in the series should the author decide to write more. Wynn Cabot is a remarkable protagonist that I would love to read more about.—Online Book Club

Praise for *Side Hustle*:

Side Hustle is an intricate mystery novel concerning missing art and murders; its heroine is compelling.—*Foreword* Clarion Reviews

Prologue

"But Santa Fe, André," she'd said when he told her he was leaving the Bureau, "...and then Napa and..." And he'd said, "That's why I wanted us to talk about it." Us. He'd said, "...us to talk about it."

What did that mean? That he wanted her to work with him in New Orleans, where he was going to set up a private investigating firm? Did it mean more? What was he asking, or was he asking anything at all?

She thought back to Santa Fe, to when they'd met. He wasn't used to someone with dyslexia; someone like her, whose brain looked at puzzles in 3-D rather than linearly, as he did. He was, she thought, maybe the most linear thinker she'd ever met. A real "if and then" guy.

To her, the world wasn't built that way—she saw life as a giant game of Jenga; its pieces delicately balanced on each other to build the whole—and by the end of their time together in Santa Fe, he'd come to appreciate her worldview.

But first, there was the beginning.

Chapter One

October 26

At Interpol headquarters Edouard Doucet swung his feet off his desk and sat up, studying more closely the latest Sotheby's auction results. What had his attention, indeed what alarmed him, was the hammer price of a piece he had never expected to see—a piece that hadn't existed for more than one hundred and fifty years.

For some reason, he'd seen the piece not once this year, here in the Sotheby's listing, but three times—the long-lost *bulto*, the Zuni San Gabriel, had knocked down at $75,500 at last Saturday evening's auction in London, bought by a church, though not the poor parish from which it had disappeared more than a century and a half before. And a bargain, even at that price.

There had been only one authentic Zuni San Gabriel—a handsome piece that had been one of a pair stolen from a New Mexico church in 1880, yet purportedly burned in a fire that had occurred fifteen years earlier. That the thing kept surfacing this year seemed more than a striking coincidence.

He began to grind his teeth—a habit he'd tried for years to break, but it had embedded itself so deeply that he did it unconsciously.

Could it be that the wealthy Zurich collector who had purchased a San Gabriel last February was selling it? No—Doucet checked the paperwork—this lot was from another owner, and so its attribution had to be called into question.

Perhaps this one came from a museum in New York—the piece everyone in the art world had believed was surely the genuine Zuni San Gabriel risen from the ashes when the museum bought it in May? He turned to a desk piled high with files on missing works of art—more than twenty thousand such files had accrued since Interpol began tracking stolen and missing artifacts in 1995—and leafed through a stack of eight or so folders, consulting dates and places of sale. And no, again.

He massaged his five o'clock shadow, considerable since five o'clock had passed four hours ago, groped for his phone and glanced at the time—two hours before the close of business in the U.S. He selected the number he wanted from the phone's directory and hit *call*.

At the office of the FBI's Art Crimes Team in Washington, D.C., André Bishop stood at the window, watching rain snarl traffic on Pennsylvania Avenue. If he didn't leave now, he would have to wait out rush hour and leave late. As he threw two full file folders into his briefcase, his cell phone buzzed. He checked the screen and cocked an eyebrow, recognizing the number that came up: Edouard Doucet at Interpol in Lyon, France, was calling—a former classmate at the Sorbonne's Institut d'Art et d'Archéologie, a man who never called just to pass the time of day.

He smiled to himself. After the Isabella Stewart Gardner debacle more than twenty years ago, perhaps the FBI's Art Crimes unit had finally redeemed itself in the eyes of the art world. Or perhaps Interpol, which had no police powers of its own, needed some muscle in the U.S. He swiped the screen with a thumb. *"Bonjour, mon ami,"* he said into the phone. *"Ça va?"*

Chapter Two

When Wynn left him, Phillip Cabot had been baffled—astonished was more the word. Until the moment she drove away, he'd thought she was bluffing. Still, she hadn't gone far, and Cabot thought that encouraging, setting herself up in a high-rise condo just down Houston's Allen Parkway from the Cabot's red-brick digs with its twelve white columns arrayed across the front veranda.

He knew his general lack of attention to her—he'd spent little time with her over the course of their five-year marriage—along with the occasional doses of clap he brought home were the reasons she'd left.

Though he felt sure he loved her, this damned "mid-life crisis" had taken a firm hold on his libido and wouldn't let go. He hadn't laughed since she'd walked out—a bar chuckle now and then, but nothing like the way he and Wynn had once laughed together. And he hadn't set foot in a kitchen, either. He and Wynn had enjoyed cooking together—their shared love of Tex-Mex fare being what brought them together—symbolic, somehow, of their passion. Since she'd left, the young women Cabot dated only made him crave the mind and body of his wife again. The most recent of these vacuous piglets had been dumber than a can of paint, and so the time had come, he decided, to try to talk Wynn into moving home. Without her, he was afraid of becoming invisible.

On Tuesday afternoon, when he stopped by her condo building armed with as much patience as he could muster—and Cabot was not a patient man—the doorman refused to announce that Cabot was in the lobby. He was noncommittal about the whereabouts of the missus until Cabot pulled out his money clip. For a twenty, the doorman admitted she wasn't home. For twenty more, he said she'd taken a suitcase. It cost Cabot two more Jacksons before the guy admitted she'd been gone for a couple of days and that she was driving.

Then came the call from Tripp, Cabot's attorney, saying that the D.A.'s office was looking for him but wouldn't divulge why. They wanted to talk to Cabot himself.

Tripp hinted at a problem with the city, too. And then he said he'd had an odd call from the FBI. That it would be better if Cabot wasn't around for a while. That maybe he should skedaddle.

Cabot headed to the AmEx office, zig-zagging between slower-moving cars along Allen Parkway and accelerating around traffic stopped at a red light while he ruminated on why the city and the Feds were on the hunt: he'd displaced several families recently to clear the land for his new strip center on the outskirts of Houston, virtually swindling those folks out of their homes. He'd bribed a Houston city councilman to change his zoning vote so Cabot could build the project. And then there was that thing with the gun shop. Which of those had caught up with him?

Cabot counted on his tall, blonde good looks at a time like this—he'd sweet-talk the little sugar behind the American Express desk into telling him where Wynn had gone. All it took was a scant fifteen minutes of Cabot's cooing for the woman to bend the rules and tell him where Wynn was running up her charge card: she'd gone to Dallas—probably, Cabot thought, to see an old sorority sister from her days at SMU—and then it looked from the gas and restaurant charges as though she was on her way to Lubbock to see her mother. She wasn't planning to stay in Lubbock long, however; she'd made a reservation at Vista Cielo Resort and Spa just outside of Santa Fe for Thursday.

He knew the hotel—a down-at-the-heels golf resort beyond the northwestern edge of town. At this point in its life, Vista Cielo needed more than a coat of paint and new carpeting to see it through the next few years—those kinds of places usually needed both a substantial face-lift and a salacious scandal involving a celebrity or a couple of murders to bring them back into the thousand-dollar-a-night fold.

Even so, the hotel's golf course was tolerable, and their booze was cheap.

In any event, a vacation was in order, and while he was at AmEx, he found a seat on a charter flight out of Houston Executive that arrived in Santa Fe about three that afternoon. He would get to Vista Cielo a full day before his wife did and give her a little surprise.

Back at the house, he threw a few clothes in a suitcase and then reached into his desk, adding to the pile of clothes his Smith and Wesson pistol and the separation papers he'd had Tripp draw up six months before. His wife could leave him all she wanted, but if she wasn't going to agree to come home, then by damn, he would be the one to cut the cord.

By Cabot's reckoning, a man on vacation needed two things: a drink in his hand and a nose for trouble. He prided himself on being able to kick up a pretty good frog froth, and well, hell, the words "trouble on vacation" were almost a foregone conclusion, weren't they? Especially in New Mexico.

He rounded a corner from Vista Cielo's lobby into its bar, lit so dimly that the place seemed for a moment completely dark. He squinted, trying to read the room while he slid onto a tooled-leather barstool. Above, palm fans circled lazily at either end of the bar's ceiling, stirring together the odors of stale beer and *chile verde*.

Cabot was hungry for trouble—midnight-snack hungry, wolf hungry—because, Chicken-fried Christ on a cracker, being the simpering fop his wife had decided she wanted for a husband didn't come close to that edge he craved, a life like he imagined the skinhead freak sitting at the opposite end of the long oak bar lived, the dude down there with the nasty-looking soul patch on his chin and what looked like a flaming skull tattooed on one bulging bicep.

Cabot ordered two fingers of Gentleman Jack, neat, and while he drank he sized up the barman—a skinny kid with a wispy, child-molester moustache on his upper lip.

The bartender pointed. "You want another?"

Cabot wet his lips. "I'm looking for something more… satisfying."

The kid waited, not saying anything.

Cabot withdrew his money clip from his jacket pocket and peeled off a hundred-dollar bill. "Something livelier than this place."

It neared sunset by the time Cabot rented a black Cadillac Escalade at the hotel's front desk and pulled out of the parking lot, the sky coloring gold from the San Pedro peaks across Los Alamos and Bandelier, setting the adobes down in Santa Fe aglow before the sun spread its embers up the mountainside. He glanced at the bartender's directions—away from town on the road that paralleled the Chama River. He topped a hill and headed down the canyon into darkness.

Alejandra was a good-looking woman for her age, Cabot thought. He gave her an appraising glance as he snapped on his Rolex—roughly forty-five, he guessed, with a sweet round face and big, dark Jennifer Lopez eyes. She had been worth more than she asked: pliable in many ways and not afraid of pain. She had massive tits, a nice cache of toys, and a stash of good ganja. Her place was a mess—he'd never seen such chaos—but the woman was a hellion in the hay.

He gestured to the wooden carving that stood on her nightstand. "Nice statue you got there. My wife likes those things, too. You want to sell it?" He pulled out his money clip.

Alejandra scoffed. "It's a *bulto*. A *santo* of Saint Jude—the *patrón* of lost causes."

She rolled over and fingered the waves of wooden flame that spread from the *bulto's* head. "See the fire of the Holy Spirit? When things get bad, you know? Like when you're having a really terrible day or something? That's when you call on Saint Jude."

She'd had the *bulto* for more than forty years. Saint Jude had gotten her through some bad times—the deaths of her mother and her brother, the birth of her children and then losing them to her lover when she became addicted to heroin, her recovery from that addiction. Through all that Saint Jude had been at her side.

CHAPTER TWO

Cabot glanced at the *bulto* and raised an eyebrow. The original man with his hair on fire.

"Sometimes he will only help at the last moment." Alejandra dropped her arm, running a finger between Cabot's legs and up to his crotch. "Anyway, he is not for sale."

Not for sale. She would sell her body, Cabot thought, but not her damn statue. "Okay. Look, there's other action around here, isn't there?"

Alejandra pulled a rumpled sheet around her, riffled the edges of five one-hundred dollar bills under the lamp base, and smiled appreciatively. "There is whatever you want, for money." She smiled. "Whatever you want except Saint Jude."

"A cockfight."

"That's no big deal." Alejandra giggled. "Around here, cockfighting is like going to a Lobos football game."

Cabot held up another fifty. "Know where I can find one or not?"

"*Si*. Of course."

"Write it down," he said and slid another fifty onto the pile of cash he'd left under the lamp.

Chapter Three

Chasing an anonymous 9-1-1 tip just after ten that evening, Cruz County sheriff's deputy DaShaye Williams arrived at the clapboard bungalow outside of town to find Alejandra Ramirez's bloody body on the floor in the small back bedroom, her head at an unnatural angle. He knew this woman, knew what she did for a living, and he knew that his boss knew her better.

He studied the room: no diamond jewelry, no fur coat, and he'd seen her wear both. He expanded his search to the rest of the small, cluttered house, but found nothing that told him how Alejandra Ramirez had been murdered, though surely, from everything he saw, she had.

Cruz County Sheriff Ordierno Feliz's headlights picked out an open gas station flanked by a row of low adobe houses, the station's windows decorated for Halloween with cardboard black cats, a jack o'lantern, and a four-foot skeleton. The holiday was less than a week away. Inside, the place sold ice cream, phone cards imprinted with an image of the Virgin of Guadelupe, and bourbon, most of it cheap.

Feliz pulled a dusty quart of Old Overholt from the back of the display and took it to the cash register. He flashed his badge and waited for the kid behind the counter to tell him the whiskey was gratis. Instead, the boy charged him full boat for the bottle—thirty bucks—and Feliz grudgingly laid the cash on the counter. Apparently professional courtesies to lawmen hadn't yet found traction in the outer reaches of Cruz County.

The bottle of rye would lubricate checkbooks when he returned to the

CHAPTER THREE

political fund-raiser he'd just left. He would wrap up his appearance at the murder scene as quickly as he could and get back to the company of the green-bellied gringos and *chuco suaves*, their wallets fat as quails.

He smoothed his black velveteen sport coat, picked two pieces of imaginary lint from impeccably-creased pants, climbed back behind the wheel of his patrol car and rolled on down the hill to a house he knew well, parking behind the two county vehicles already at the scene.

Inside the front door, evidence markers jumbled with the mess of dirty dishes, dirty laundry, and dirty magazines. Why was it that murder always occurred in the middle of chaos? Why not in some place with clean bathrooms and polished floors?

At least the body didn't stink yet.

Feliz stepped over Alejandra, kicked an evidence marker out of the way, and leaned against a wall.

Squatting next to the medical examiner, Deputy DaShaye Williams glanced up at Feliz and tsk'ed. "You're contaminating the crime scene."

Feliz studied Williams's African-American face for a moment. Feliz thought Williams was a good deputy, but the man was a hard-ass when it came to detail. Everything by the book, nothing left to gut instinct or human nature. Feliz hadn't risen through the ranks by following the book; he had built a career based on nothing more than following leads based on hunches. He took comfort in the thought that he knew people—especially women, knew them better than he knew regulations. And he sure as hell wasn't going to take criticism from a deputy—especially not this guy who had decided that he, too, was qualified to be sheriff of Cruz County and mounted a rival campaign. Williams was rank and file, and that was all he'd ever be, no matter how squeaky clean he wanted to play it.

Feliz checked his gold Cartier watch. "You took me away from a nice dinner to come look at this? Give me the details."

The details so far were, according to Williams, that a phone call from an anonymous male individual was received by the 9-1-1 dispatcher; that the caller reported the body of a female at this address, and that Williams, thinking the address might mean something to Feliz, had telephoned him right away.

Which was one cause for Feliz's irritation. As sheriff, he shouldn't be called away from his personal time to investigate the death of a whore. Even this one. "You thought the address might mean something to me?"

"Alejandra Ramirez. You knew her, I think."

Feliz shrugged. "In a professional capacity, yes." And although he hadn't, he would have liked to know her in a biblical sense, too. "I met her when I was working those trafficking cases three years ago. She… proved useful several times."

That was the other source of his irritation: that this hooker, a woman who had been among the few he might count as his friend—or, perhaps, merely an ally—had been killed. Despite that—or even because of it—Feliz thought bringing him into the investigation could have waited until morning, couldn't it? Glancing down at the medical examiner, still bent over Alejandra's body, he said, "Jesus, Jackson, you look like hell."

The ME, his eyes and skin as ashen as his gray hair, gave a cynical chuckle. "I was in bed."

Feliz sneered. "At this time of the evening? Don't tell me guys like you get lucky too." He looked again at Alejandra Ramirez's body and winced. "Do you need me here? Really?"

"I have to get her back to the lab and get some X-rays. Then get blood and tissue samples in for analysis. Don't think you'd be much use."

"Well, don't fall asleep on the job. The way you look, they'd toe tag you and lock you in a freezer." Feliz smacked the ME on the back jovially and laughed at his own joke.

Jackson didn't laugh. "Looks like the cause of death was a blow with a blunt instrument. Her skull is crushed on the left side, meaning the killer was right-handed. Unless, of course, he hit her from behind."

"You're sure it was a man?"

Jackson sighed. "With victims like this…"

"Like what?"

"May be alcohol involved, may be drugs, but always a man."

The ME stood, and Williams stood with him. "One break," Williams said.

CHAPTER THREE

"The caller said he saw a black Cadillac Escalade with a rental-car bar code in the window leave the scene. I'll go roust the car-rental people."

Williams and Jackson walked outside. Through the open front door, Feliz could see the ME's wagon and Williams's patrol car in the road, their lights flashing, illuminating neighbors who craned their necks to see however much they might see.

If Feliz was going to keep DaShaye Williams at bay in the upcoming election, he'd have to take the lead in this investigation, spending precious time finding the killer of a prostitute when he could be doing more worthwhile things like prying money and votes from the innocents who supported him. He'd worked too hard and come too far back to be dragged down by this shit. Feliz stepped over the body and looked down at Alejandra Ramirez one last time.

An ache replaced hunger in his stomach. So much of what she'd done for him were things he expected of all the hookers in his county—she contributed to his campaign to keep herself out of jail, made him feel like a man by admiring his clothes, derided his ex-wife, soothed his hurt feelings whenever life slighted him.

Feliz glanced outside: off to the right, Williams interviewed a neighborhood kid, scribbling notes diligently; Jackson was knee-deep in paperwork.

He removed a pair of latex gloves from his pants pocket and snapped them on, stepped to Alejandra's bed, and picked up a joint from the nightstand. In all the chaos, no one would miss that. He dropped the joint into his shirt pocket and turned so that he stood between the front door and the nightstand.

He frowned slightly. Something else used to occupy a place on Alejandra's bedside table, something that had left an oval void in the dust. He lifted the lamp slightly, hoping he would find what he felt for and—yes. Alejandra had said she always had her clients put her fees and tips under the lamp. He doubled five one-hundred dollar bills and a fifty into the palm of his hand and set the lamp back in place. To hell with fingerprints and chain of evidence. Alejandra Ramirez had just made her last, and biggest, donation to his campaign fund.

She would have wanted him to have money, enough to cover some last-minute campaign signs. Signs with a large picture of his face on the left and to the right, in outsized letters, the call to action:

Re-elect Ordierno
FELIZ
Cruz County Sheriff

His opponent, DaShaye Williams, his own deputy, the nerdy cop who had the balls to run against him, was going down. This time, Feliz wasn't going to let his re-election get away.

Phillip Cabot combed the back of his hair into place, slid from behind the wheel of the black Cadillac Escalade, checked his fly, walked across the drive to Vista Cielo's main entrance, and left the keys on the valet stand.

This trip might turn out pretty damn fine after all, he thought. He and Alejandra had done some unusual things. Not to mention he'd gotten away from that whole mess in Houston and spent a couple hours at a damn fine cockfight, which had been almost as good a high as Alejandra's grass. The cocks had been well-trained, armed, and drugged into a frenzy by the time the crowd cleared a space for the battle. He'd watched four bouts, two of them lasting more than ten minutes, all of them ending with dead birds. Between fights, he passed around a joint Alejandra had given him and fended off a pickpocket. Only one of his bets had paid off, and that, combined with the extra he'd spent to stand close enough to get blood and feathers on his Fendi loafers, meant he'd dropped a packet on the evening.

But what the hell, he reasoned, what the fuck's it for if not to play with? Like the guy he saw headed down toward Alejandra's just as he'd left—some dude in a metal-flake gold Corvette. He'd love to know who that was—probably another hotel guest sent out there by the bartender. Whoever he was, he and that sonofabitch had this in common: they both knew how to burn through some mighty cash.

Chapter Four

The clock on his nightstand read 2:17 a.m. when Seamus Caine's phone vibrated. Enveloped in the vague dread that accompanies a call at that time of night, he propped himself up in bed and stared at the phone, scooting along the surface of the table as it hummed.

Still, he was awake—he had just begun his day. He grabbed up the phone and swiped the screen. "What now?"

André Bishop grimaced. Seamus Caine was an unsurpassed authority when it came to the questions Bishop had tonight—Caine knew more about art than anyone else Bishop had ever met, including curators and archaeologists of every stripe. His depth of knowledge encompassed everything from Stone Age artifacts to contemporary art, but his specialty focused on monstrances and religious triptychs. He had been of great help in solving many of the FBI's cases, but he wasn't the warmest of human beings.

Though it neared 2:30 in the morning, he knew Caine would be awake. Bishop pinched the bridge of his nose, trying to wake himself up. He resented having to lose any of the small amount of sleep he normally got to make this phone call, but if you wanted to talk to Seamus Caine you did what he asked—you called between two and four AM, and you made it brief. Caine had always slept in sync with the French—a rhythm that suited his body better than trying to keep up with the vagaries of jet lag and time changes when he flew between his beloved France and the U.S.

He acknowledged with a grunt Bishop's explanation that the FBI would be the liaison between Interpol and local authorities to investigate the strange reappearance and apparent forgeries of the Zuni San Gabriel *bulto*. "Dear boy, you do understand the impossibility of the real Zuni San Gabriel, don't you? That it purportedly burned in the Smithsonian fire?"

"The big one, in eighteen-sixty-five. Yes."

"Does it not strike you as strange that the *bulto* wasn't put into the collection until eighteen-eighty but was destroyed in the Smithsonian's fire fifteen years prior?"

"So we're looking for something that's charred?"

"You're not listening. You're looking for something that might never have existed. A grail, if you will. *Une revenant.* A ghost."

"The nineteenth-century version of an urban legend."

"Maybe… if it ever was real. But there were some who said they saw it *in situ* before it was spirited away, you'll pardon the pun, to the Smithsonian, and then it is worth a very great deal of money."

"Or," Bishop croaked, still groggy, "it may be impossible to distinguish between the real and the fake. Then whatever reasons you have for valuing the real Zuni San Gabriel must also exist for the fake. The two pieces would have equal value."

On his end, Caine nodded. Bishop had a point. The pieces coming on the market might be old forgeries—an exciting idea. If they were, say, from 1900 or so, then they could still have considerable value. But he held a trump card in this conversation. Small wonder the FBI had fumbled the Isabella Stewart Gardner investigation if this was an example of their short-sightedness.

Caine picked up Alice, his King Charles spaniel, and nuzzled her neck. The old dog had craved constant attention ever since Gertrude, her elder sister, had passed away two months before. Then he said into the phone, "Or, the fakes might have more value, had you thought of that? Consider this—whatever quality the real Zuni San Gabriel has, the fake is replicating that so well it's apparently indistinguishable from the real thing. That alone means that the pieces should have equal value. However, the fake has something the original does not—it is *trying* to have those qualities. Think about it—there's no real value in something being what it naturally is. Who is really surprised when a Stradivarius sounds good? On the other

CHAPTER FOUR

hand, if a fake sounds as good as a Stradivarius, that is something impressive. So a fake Zuni San Gabriel may have more value than the real thing—it has all the qualities of the real thing, plus the additional quality of transcending its natural limitations and taking on the greater role of something else."

Bishop was in no mood for Caine's lofty crap. "Who," he rasped, "who can you think of who can help me with this one? Your best authenticator of *santos*—who would that be?"

"A very special woman, Bishop—and so if I lend her to the FBI, I want you to watch her." He paused again to let Bishop know he was serious. "Her name is Wynn Cabot, and, oddly, she is on her way to Santa Fe—should be there later today. Saves the FBI an airfare, eh? She's very, very good at these things. Very knowledgeable. I taught her myself. None better than Wynn. But I'm telling you, any harm comes to her, there will be problems, *c'est compris?*"

Excellent, Bishop thought, *excellent*. He had a standing invitation with an expensive hooker who lived on the outskirts of Santa Fe—a woman who could satisfy every longing a government employee might dream up, and he had dreamed up some new ones since he'd seen her last. They were humdingers. A trip to Santa Fe wouldn't be any imposition at all.

Chapter Five

Neron Diaz sat once more at the far end of the long oak bar, his line of sight directly out the doorway and across the lobby of the Vista Cielo Resort and Spa. He wanted—no, he needed—another drink, but at the moment, the bartender had found something more interesting than tending bar: a leggy blonde three stools down, a real crowd-pleaser, equipped with some imposing day diamonds and a dialed-up set of knockers. A promising adventure for whoever might be lucky enough to mount an assault on those *chalupas*.

Diaz tried to concoct an opener, but his timing felt off, whether from the unexpected October heat wave or the damned mariachi music blaring from the restaurant next door—"Ayy-yi-yi-yi…"—or from the three double-shot tequilas he'd downed in the last hour. Before he could come up with something clever, the blonde threw down a twenty for one margarita and took off on the arm of a short Latino, leaving a bottle rocket lit in Diaz's pants.

A television over the bar played an old Mexican children's program starring a red-headed clown named Niko Liko. Canned laughter swelled and faded over the screech of an accordion.

He scratched at the soul patch on his chin while he sized up a woman who stood at the front desk. Good looking redhead. Fit. Nice ass. If he weren't on his way to being drunk as a dacked mackerel, he might go make a play for her. He'd seen her before, checking in with Pablo Estrella, so he knew she had connections.

He wondered what El Eché might know about the woman and how grateful

CHAPTER FIVE

he might be to know she'd just shown up in Santa Fe. He pulled out his cell phone.

Chapter Six

The New Mexico sun highlighted scars on the backs of Eliu Colón's arms, faded ridges and furrows that crosshatched the hotel manager's arms from the hems of his short-sleeved shirt to his wrists.

Wynn Cabot frowned. The result of some freak accident? Some childhood prank gone wrong? She'd seen Colón many times behind the desk at Vista Cielo—why hadn't she noticed the scars before? He was an odd little man, she thought—though he looked friendly enough, he was distant and unwelcoming, never willing to meet her gaze, peculiar traits for a front-desk job.

She lifted her eyes to the mirror behind the reception desk and studied its reflection of the gift shop behind her. In the mirror, she saw a hand reach into the window of the shop to remove a *bulto* from the display and present it to a customer. The customer took the statue, and the movement was so familiar…she knew that arm, the top of that head. She gasped. *No, not now.*

She turned in slow motion, but by the time her line of sight fastened on the gift shop rather than its reflection, both the owner of the hand and the man who looked like Pablo Estrella were gone. Disoriented, she could hear her heart beat in her ears.

"*Hola, Señora* Cabot," Eliu Colón called to her. "I will be with you in two minutes."

Wynn wasn't sure what she had seen in the mirror behind the reception desk. It was all backwards, of course, and not from her sporadic dyslexia; this time things truly seemed out of place. The mirror's heavy silver frame

CHAPTER SIX

caught the afternoon sun, almost obscuring the reflection in the looking glass itself: terra-cotta tiles, faded blue-and-yellow upholstery on the oversized lobby sofas, lush potted plants, striped fabric billowing at the windows with the rise of afternoon *vientes*. The lobby of Vista Cielo was reversed, but more than that, she saw the bright, disjointed images as pieces of a puzzle she felt a need to put together.

"So," Colón sighed. "We welcome you again, *Señora* Cabot."

She smiled and slid her American Express card across the counter. "It's good to be back. A room near the pool if you have it."

Colón busied himself making a card key while he debated—should he tell her that her husband had checked in yesterday? Maybe she already knew that. Should he whisper to her that Pablo Estrella had arrived this morning? He didn't think Mrs. Cabot foolish enough to set up that kind of circumstance. He was almost sure she didn't know Estrella was there—or that he knew of her presence. Let the lovers discover each other for themselves.

He shook his head. It was a shame, he thought, what Vista Cielo Resort and Spa had become in recent years—a refuge for those acquainted with blackmail, betrayal, and bankruptcy. Yet the hotel's staff was discreet in all things—everyone had an expectation of privacy.

He handed her a room-key envelope while he glared over the top of his glasses. "I hope you enjoy your stay, Mrs. Cabot. You always do."

Phillip Cabot signed his afternoon bar tab, looked up, and paused, seeing, through the door of the bar, his wife at the front desk. She looked good—her red hair curling over her shoulders, her figure as trim as it was when he'd first met her seven years ago. He wasn't in the mood to confront her yet. He'd had one too many Gentleman Jacks while he watched highlights of old Houston Oilers games—damn, but Bum Phillips had been a good coach—and he needed to get his blood pressure under control.

She wouldn't be happy he'd come, he knew that, just as he was pretty sure she'd be really pissed to find out they were going to share a room for a few days. He smiled to himself—he'd taken a few pains to make sure she didn't know he was her roommate until he was ready to reveal himself and the little second honeymoon he had planned: he'd wiped the sink clean after his morning shave, stashed his dop kit in the bottom drawer of the bathroom counter, and shoved his small suitcase under the king-sized bed. At the end of their little honeymoon, he would take a knee and ask her to come home. If she said no, he'd give her the separation agreement, ready for her signature. It would be interesting to see what she did then, if it came to that. The separation invoked their prenup—she'd be a pauper.

First, though, he would take a walk, settle his thoughts, get himself right.

Wynn Cabot had the bellman stow one bag in the closet and set the other on a luggage stand. After the bellman left, she changed into a swimsuit and cover-up and stepped out onto the patio that adjoined the swimming pool, into the line of sight of two men.

Chapter Seven

Weeks had passed while Pablo Estrella tried to set up a meeting with someone, anyone, who might introduce him to a new market for the work he was selling—he'd pulled strings, called favors, phoned distant contacts. But his reputation and prison record preceded him—private collectors and curators from the museums stayed at least an arm's length away. He needed a sale—he was out of money and almost out of resources.

In the end, and with cajoling, state senator Lisa Guzman had agreed to have a look at what he had, but with conditions: she wanted to see only work with provenance, and whatever meeting they had must be in a public place.

The senator was a powerful woman—the senate's majority whip in Santa Fe. She'd sat on the board of the Museum of International Folk Art for many years, and the boards of the Opera and Saint John's College as well. She had contacts. Wealthy contacts. A sale would take a while longer through the senator, but he'd take who he could get.

Estrella had stumbled onto the forgeries market at a time when his life as an antiquities dealer hadn't panned out as well as he'd expected and, after serving a short sentence for trafficking and money laundering down in Las Cruces, he'd done well in this new life, almost as though it had chosen him. This way of doing things—using his knowledge of *santos* and remaining just this side of the law paid off handsomely, when it paid off at all. It had gotten him out of debt and enabled him to live like a human being again. It wasn't easy, this life, though he dealt with a better class of people. He'd deemed what he was doing respectable until he met Wynn Cabot, and then lost her when she found out how he really made his money.

He had thought Wynn beautiful from the moment they first met—what? Almost a year ago. That mass of red hair, her pale skin, her green eyes, all pretty, of course, but her body—*Madré de Dios*, those breasts, that rump, her muscular back. A swimmer's body, she had said on the afternoon they first made love. But she could do so much more than swim with that lovely body. He loved her, this fiery woman from Houston. She made him laugh; he liked who he became when he was around her.

He stepped out on his balcony and leaned his forearms on the railing, taking in the familiar view: Vista Cielo's two-story main building surrounded the pool on three sides, its balconies hanging almost directly over the water. On the fourth side, the dining terrace spread out in a fan so that guests had their choice of eating in the sun or in the shade under the balconies. He stared for a moment at the pool, squinting into the sunset.

Was it? Could it be? Or was this wishful thinking, since this was where they'd spent so much time together?

He watched Wynn spread a towel out on a chaise, an angular sliver of late sun doing what he could not—touching her shoulder and caressing her hair. She dove from the edge of the pool into the deep end, and glided swiftly from end to end. He knew she would do forty laps, knew it as well as he knew her voice and the lemon scent of her hair.

Watching her swim plunged him into the hope that filled his mind every time he thought of her: he would change; he'd start over, again. In an honest line of business. If Wynn would only come back to him.

Wynn had just stepped from the pool and toweled off when her phone chimed. She looked at the screen and frowned. "Hello?"

"Can you talk?"

His voice washed over her, tumbled down the weeks and months since she'd heard it last. "I shouldn't," she said.

"Look up, across the courtyard."

She lifted her gaze from the pool. "What are you doing here, Pablo?"

Chapter Eight

"I came at the last minute. I got a call the day before yesterday. Senator Guzman has agreed to see me for dinner tonight. She might open up a new distribution network.... Wynn, come up to my room, please." From his balcony, he held his arms out to her.

"That's not a good idea." *You deceived me. I loved you, and you deceived me.* She wiped her face with her towel. Her red curls stuck to her forehead and neck, a sheen of moisture obscuring the freckles that dotted her nose and cheeks, shoulders and cleavage. Beads of perspiration glistened amber at her hairline.

"Please. I will tell you everything."

She closed her eyes. Even if Pablo told her that he'd behave like a saint, seeing him would be too hard. She leaned against the adobe wall and waited, thinking nothing, remembering everything.

"I have an idea," he said at last. "Meet me at the stables in twenty minutes—a chance encounter between two strangers." He paused. "Or, better still, like two old friends. Yes? Like two old friends."

Odd, she thought. *Deceit comes so easily to him. Why didn't I recognize that sooner?* She sighed. "Maybe. I don't know."

"In twenty minutes. I'll wait for you."

She stepped through the gate to the stables. He stood about fifty yards away, but she would have recognized him from any distance, even backlit in the twilight as he was. How different the two men were: tall, blonde Phillip and Pablo, more nearly her height, with dark hair and deep brown eyes. And their dispositions were complete contradictions. Although Phillip could be fun and, on the surface, good company, he was demanding in private. Pablo cared deeply about his family and about the plight of the poor, but lived only in the moment. Still, both of them preferred to leave the finer points of life—humdrum daily routines and the observation of laws—to others.

She walked down a brick-paved path and stood stiffly while he embraced her, pushed him away, and stepped back.

"Easy," she said. "We're two people meeting by chance, remember?"

He nodded sheepishly. "Old friends meeting by chance—and we are. You look wonderful."

"It's always good to get away."

"But I'm surprised you chose this place. You left in such a hurry last time."

She turned toward the sunset. "It had nothing to do with the place. I needed some time alone."

"What will you do while you are here?"

"I thought that as long as I'm in the area, I might acquire some *santos*"—she looked at him—"legitimately."

He toyed with a small tumbleweed at his feet until a breeze whisked it away. "That's what I never got the chance to tell you, last time...before you left. That I would change in a moment, for you."

Wynn snorted and turned away, watching the last of the sunset.

Taking her shoulders, Pablo buried his nose in her hair, smelling again the lemon scent he remembered. "I haven't stolen since I saw you last, and I don't plan to. I'm going out to Arco Viejo tomorrow to look at the workshop of a *santero* there—a man named Ignacio Garza. A client of mine wants to distribute *santos* in museum gift shops throughout the U. S. It's a legitimate job for everyone. Once I see that the *bultos* and *retablos* are good enough—and I expect I will—the distributor will begin shipping here in the Southwest, then across Texas and into Arizona and California. Garza and his workers stand to make quite a bit of money."

"If they don't cut quality to keep production up," she said over her shoulder. "I've seen it happen before."

"Come back to me, Wynn. We can help these people out of their poverty. I

CHAPTER EIGHT

can make up for what I did."

Wynn looked again at the fading sky. Could men change? Change quickly if they wanted to? If he'd really reformed, she—they—could do a lot of good. She turned abruptly to avoid the kiss she knew was coming and said, "I'll think about it."

Phillip Cabot watched the two of them from the top of the brick path. Had she come to Vista Cielo to meet this guy, then? How naïve he'd been to think she would hang around a place like this by herself. It changed nothing, though, except the sequence of events. He was still her husband—for the moment—and maybe she would have to deal with that now rather than in a few days. He would give her his ultimatum at dinner tonight and make his surprise visit complete.

Chapter Nine

Wynn ran her key card in the slot, snapped open the hotel room door, and gave a yelp.

Phillip sat out on the patio marking a racing form.

Her mind raced—of course, he had the resources to find her. He'd probably had her followed from the minute she'd left him last year. But why would he care? Why a sudden appearance here, and why now? He'd changed in the last couple of years—was it a phase? Was it true when the marriage counselor warned her about mid-life crises? Was the crisis perhaps over?

She slipped out of her sandals, opened a bottle of water, stepped out onto the patio, and sat down in a chair beside his before she spoke. "The obvious question, of course, is why are you here, Phillip?"

Cabot dropped the racing form and pencil on the concrete slab, crossed his feet at the ankles, and folded his hands across his stomach. "Because I came to see you at your condo and found out you were gone, that's why. I want to talk to you."

"There's a twist."

"I thought maybe since your lease is almost up, you might think about coming home."

"Are you more concerned about my lease term or about who is going to be on your arm at the Hunts' annual do?"

He gave her his most sincere smile—the smile he reserved for closing deals, for conning golf bets, for getting women into bed. "We belong together, Wynn. We deserve each other."

"No, Phillip, I don't deserve you."

CHAPTER NINE

"Now, darlin', don't sell yourself short."

Wynn snorted a laugh. "Far from selling myself short, I deserve far better than you've delivered for years. I think I'll renew my lease."

"Wynn, you don't know what you're saying. Do yourself a favor and come home."

She rose, crossed to the phone on the desk, and hit 0. "*Sí, hola Señor* Colón, I wonder if you could have a bellman move Mr. Cabot's things to another room, *por favor*? He will not be staying in the room I reserved."

She paused, hearing Colón's voice directing a bellman. "You will have to ask *him* how long he plans to stay. As you'll recall when I made my reservation, I asked for a quiet room, a single room. Mr. Cabot was not included for a reason."

Cabot stood, walked to the bed, pulled out his suitcase, and reached into it—but paused before he pulled out the separation agreement. There was—there always had been—something about Wynn that bound him to her. He saw that thing in her eyes that made men write love songs. He admired her energy, her independence. She didn't need him—a fact that delighted and irritated him in equal proportion. Still, she hadn't brought the guy from the stables back to her room, nor had she gone somewhere with him. Cabot didn't know what gave with her, but he thought he'd try to find out—even though she was running him off. He would stick around another day or so.

Road-weary, FBI Agent André Bishop checked into a Budget Inn Express on Santa Fe's Cerrillos Road, a marginal hotel with a reasonable government rate, and called the only 505 area code telephone number he had bothered to store on his phone. He had tried to reach the woman twice on his trip from D.C. to New Mexico, and the result was the same as on the previous calls: no ring on the other end, no answering machine, no recording saying the number had been disconnected. Nothing but dead silence.

At five-thirty, he shaved, splashed on an overabundance of Axe aftershave, and drove out to Vista Cielo for his six-o'clock meeting with Wynn Cabot. When he saw the woman who walked across the lobby, he gasped. There were times when he hated his job and times when the FBI could pay him half the salary he made for doing what he did, and he'd do it gladly. The next hour, he could tell, was going to be one of the latter. Seamus Caine had said she was smart, but he hadn't said what a lot of woman she was. No wonder Caine was concerned about sending a stranger to see her.

Wynn glanced sidelong at Bishop as she tried to study the Sotheby's auction results he'd spread before her on the lobby coffee table. She frowned and blinked, trying to order the information in her head. Her dyslexia kicked up when she was stressed, and the print on the catalog pages was small—even in normal circumstances, she had trouble with small fonts and fine print. Not quite a learning disability, but certainly not normal.

She hadn't been pleased when Caine called the day before to tell her that the FBI had contacted him, looking for an on-site authority to discuss the multiple appearances of the famous Zuni San Gabriel *bulto*. By late in the day today, men popping up in her life like whack-a-moles had ratcheted up the jumble in her head. She knew—*knew*—that the FBI agent was waiting for some sort of sage pronouncement from her about the recent coincidences surrounding the *bulto*.

Now, here she was, working. Trying to work. Bishop made her nervous—he leaned in too close when he spoke. Was wearing some kind of godawful aftershave. A pleasant-looking guy, in an average-brown-hair-brown-shoes-and-Timex sort of way. Twice he had reached across to touch her arm or her back. Each time she'd moved farther down the sofa when he did so, until she'd reached the armrest and was trapped. There was also something odd about his breathing; he made a gurgling nasal sound as though he had hay fever. Still, he worked in Art Crimes for the FBI—the man wasn't a fool, and he had to have some art background or he wouldn't be sitting here.

She's aloof, this one, Bishop thought. None prettier, but a real goofball, acting like she didn't understand what he'd shown her. And there was something up with her eyes—she kept squinting and frowning and rubbing her forehead. Maybe she couldn't see well, or maybe she had a headache. He kept trying to

CHAPTER NINE

explain the different Sotheby's sales of the same—yet not the same—piece, but she didn't seem to understand why Interpol and the FBI were at all concerned. He doubted she was as smart as Caine claimed.

Wynn wasn't comfortable with any of this. Special Agent André Bishop had presented what looked like FBI credentials, but she'd been so rattled about Pablo's sudden appearance, and then Phillip's, that when she sat down for this meeting, Bishop could have shown her a tin star from *High Noon* and she wouldn't have known the difference. All she had hoped for was to spend a few days alone at Vista Cielo, to enjoy the last of autumn in the Sangre de Cristos before winter set in—a day or so in the hotel's spa, a couple of plates of *chile rellenos*, and some time to think.

Every one of these men wanted her attention—right here, right now—and that was eerie. She fought back a sense that they had somehow all conspired together. No, she thought, her tin-foil hat was simply on too tight. Still, she sensed something stirring—something dark. Or maybe all that was dark was her mood.

Eliu Colón milled around one corner of the reception desk, organizing and reorganizing the rack of pamphlets that told of attractions in the area—river rafting, hiking, shopping. He glanced frequently out toward the dining terrace where state senator Lisa Guzman sat with Pablo Estrella.

Colón had spent countless hours with her as they grew up together in Arco Viejo—he as Ordierno Feliz's shadow, Lisa as Feliz's girlfriend—and he had never forgotten how she taunted him for the scars on his arms and on his back; she was the one who had nicknamed him "Iguanito," and the name had stuck. Everyone in Arco Viejo knew him by that name.

He despised Lisa Guzman for belittling him almost as much as he hated the control El Eché wielded over the hotel and his hometown—twin hatreds that left Colón's heart little room for loving.

Senator Guzman leaned back in her chair and pushed aside the photographs that Pablo Estrella had laid out on the table. Their dinner had been interrupted three times by people who wanted a word with her—a favor on a floor vote, a deal on a water pact, a mention in committee. She'd barely focused on Estrella and his sales pitch. She wanted to tie the meeting up before anyone else asked anything of her.

She twirled the large diamond ring on her right hand and then folded her hands and leaned across the table. "Look, I appreciate what you're doing for the churches—really, I do. I'm sure the parishes can use the occasional bump in the collection plate. But—"

"These are the real thing, Senator. They deserve to be exhibited not only at the Museum of International Folk Art but in a wider market—I would say worldwide. And the *santeros* deserve to be recognized for the artisans they are. A win-win for the churches and the history of our artisans." Estrella gestured to the pile of photographs. "I know you have constituents who would love to have one or more of these. You might broker such a sale in exchange, let's say, for a cut of the sale price."

"Ordierno Feliz..." she paused and picked up one of the photos. "You two palled around together, I think." She handed the picture to Estrella. "Feliz showed a piece similar to this one to one of the Folk Art's curators last week. The curator mentioned it to me because...well, as everyone knows, Feliz and I..."

"A similar piece? Did the curator say which one?"

"A San Gabriel, she said. Looked to her like a very good copy."

"There's more than one of those on the market. I know where they're coming from, and so do you."

"That's what I told her—that Feliz's campaign cash is apparently drying up, and he's trying to peddle new pieces as"—Guzman waggled fingers in air quotes—"collectibles."

"My San Gabriel is not from Arco Viejo."

"Some of the work that comes out of Arco Viejo is quite good, you know."

"Of course I know, and I also know that none of the others in Arco Viejo are as good as Ignacio Garza. That the others rough out the statues, and Garza finishes them. Well, apparently, he finishes *some* of them. I was out there this morning, visiting Garza's workshop. It's funny—I've never seen

CHAPTER NINE

such…such an odd assortment of work coming out of one place." Estrella paused and thought for a moment and then shook his head. "They will ruin their hands, those men, pounding on their chisels."

"I'm sure Garza is producing as many *santos* as he can before that happens," the senator said. "I've known Ignacio Garza my whole life. I can spot his *santos* at fifty paces. I'm no fool."

Estrella took in a long breath. She would have known the old *santero*—she hailed from Arco Viejo herself. He hoped she hadn't spotted the few Garza *bultos* he'd salted among the photos of the genuine collector pieces he was trying to sell her.

Lisa Guzman tossed the photos in her briefcase, snapped it shut, stood and leaned close to Estrella's ear. "All I can say is that if I find any interest, I'll be in touch. My collector pays me for the *bulto*, I take fifty percent of that price, and you pay me a finder's fee in addition. As you say, 'a win-win,' *qué no?*"

Chapter Ten

The smell of oak leaves mulching under the chamisa, piñon smoke curling against a deep blue sky, and the last of summer's apricots drying in the chilly sun infused the air over Arco Viejo. In the valley below, the sounds of a sawmill and hammers broke the silence of a late sunrise as the town's *santeros* began their day.

Two women stood in a storage shed at the back of the church property, down a slope dotted with clutches of sunflowers gone to seed. The shed held furniture, coat racks, forgotten luggage, rental skis, replacement drapes and floor tiles, and costumes for the annual *Dia de los Muertos* celebration.

The larger woman shook her head. "That's all I see up here." She dusted off her hands and climbed down from the ladder. "I have bone bread rising. It's ready for the oven."

"I'll come back later, then. Let's get these up to the house." The smaller woman turned the cart out of the building, and the two of them pushed it up the hill. "You just save some of that bone bread for me."

A moment later, they entered the parish kitchen, where three younger women sat at a prep table, curling brightly colored paper around wire stems to make flowers or carefully turning out molds of sugar skulls onto a tray. One of the women picked up a bag full of icing and began piping names onto the skulls. "I never know whose names to put on these."

The baker wiped her hands on a dishtowel. "Who died this past year?"

"Tina Vee, in that accident last May."

"We all miss Tio Rodrigo," the baker said, a far-off look in her eyes. "But he'll be back. That's the nice part about *Dia de los Muertos*. They all come

CHAPTER TEN

back."

"If you believe that stuff."

The *anciana* pushed a lock of hair out of her face, inadvertently wiping a smear of bread flour across her face. "Don't you?"

"Nope. I think when you're dead, you're dead."

"You don't think souls come back? How sad. Ah, you're just in a mood today. Tio will be here, you watch."

The younger woman piped Rodrigo's name on a sugar skull. "Someone else is dead, I hear. Alejandra Ramirez."

Talk in the kitchen went silent. Two of the women made the sign of the cross.

"Happened night before last," she went on. "Somebody killed her."

"One of her…customers?" The *anciana* cut the bread dough into portions and began shaping the pieces into bones.

"I don't know. Maybe she'll come back and tell us who did it," the woman said and giggled.

"Stop. You're making fun." The *anciana* worked her dough. "She was a sinner, Alejandra."

The woman shrugged. "Who are we to judge? We all do things we don't want to do, but we have to… for the money."

Chapter Eleven

Ordierno Feliz stepped out of the Museum of International Folk Art into a thin late-evening sun, shaking with rage. God damn Lisa Guzman—the woman had beaten him yet again, as she had time after time for the last fifteen years. Had he really thought the curator wouldn't check with Lisa before the museum spent its money on a piece he was selling?

His divorce from Lisa Guzman ten years ago had been long and highly public, covered daily on local television and in newspapers from Denver to Albuquerque, Dallas to Phoenix. Two public servants—a county sheriff and a state senator—calling each other names, leveling threats, and, on one afternoon, physically duking it out in a hair-pulling match in court until the sergeant-at-arms separated them.

In the end, a judge awarded Lisa the house, the Lexus, and everything in Feliz's bank account. He lost his campaign for re-election the following year to the asshole who had represented Lisa in their divorce, a pudgy man who had apparently decided he wasn't finished destroying Feliz's life. It had taken two years for Feliz to win back control of Cruz County, overcome the crushing debt Lisa had left him, and defeat the fucker who'd robbed him of his job, his car, his bank account, and his house.

But the curator's blow this afternoon had been the worst of it—Lisa had confirmed the curator's suspicions that far from the historical folk art Feliz represented his San Gabriel *bulto* to be, glorified with its counterfeit provenance, it was nothing but tourist-grade junk. His campaign funds were dangerously low—he'd spent the money he found under Alejandra Ramirez's

CHAPTER ELEVEN

lamp for his glorious signs, and he'd already committed the money from the museum sale for a last-minute mailing.

And to top it all off, the curator told him the museum had decided to purchase Pablo Estrella's San Gabriel instead.

Estrella had his own reasons to humiliate Feliz. In the two years after Feliz had lost his election for Cruz County Sheriff to Lisa Guzman's divorce attorney, he and Estrella had run whatever Los Sapos handed them to run across the border. Mostly heroin, sometimes cocaine. But when Feliz got wind that they were about to be hauled up on smuggling charges, he'd gone down to Las Cruces and had a chat with the local LEOs. Estrella served a stint in lockup; Feliz hit the campaign trail.

Feliz liked giving in to his anger—he felt manly standing in his rage. He thought more clearly, walked taller. He whispered thanks to Lisa Guzman and her attorney and to Pablo Estrella, squared his shoulders and, in five strides, crossed the parking lot to his patrol car.

Wynn Cabot pulled her sweater around her as she wound down the brick path to the stables. As she rounded the corner to the paddock area, Pablo Estrella stepped from the shadow of the stables and took her by the shoulders. She stopped, looked up into his eyes, and tipped her head back, waiting, wanting the kiss she had ducked the last time they met.

Instead, Estrella said, "I sold a piece today."

"What piece?"

"A San Gabriel—a wonderful old piece."

"And where did you get it, Pablo? From the church in Arco Viejo?"

Estrella sighed. He'd tried—truly tried this time, for Wynn and for his own self-esteem—to resist the easy way to make a buck, but temptation was the way he always chose. "Yes, *Padré* Hernandez was grateful for the money, and I—"

She stepped away from him. "Nothing's changed, has it, Pablo? Did you have to do that?"

"At least I'm not lying to you this time. The priest suggested I buy the piece, Wynn. Their little church needs the money so badly. And such a beautiful *bulto*—it deserves to be seen by more than a handful of parishioners once a week."

"Doesn't it bother you at all that what you took out of that village might be the only thing that fires the imagination of those people? The one piece that ties them to their God?"

"Wynn, I—"

"I haven't been to Arco Viejo—yet. But I know what you did. Honestly, Pablo, you weren't selling a piece of folk art when you did this, you were selling Arco Viejo's humanity. Don't you get it?"

"But the museum paid handsomely, and I passed half of what I made to the church—in addition to what I paid for the piece. I would rather see the museum spend its money on this kind of work than the phony *bulto* someone else had tried to sell them earlier this week."

She took three steps up the brick path and then turned. "I would hope the folks at the museum are savvy enough to avoid spending money on stolen art and bad copies." She sighed. Was every man she met a con artist, or did she just attract the type? "You're out of my life, Pablo, and this time it's for good."

Chapter Twelve

Wynn took a table for one in the dining room and picked at *huevos rancheros* while she scanned the morning newspapers: upcoming elections, a water rights feud, a gas leak last week, impending funding cuts. Then she turned to the Arts Calendar and marveled at the number of exhibits, openings, themed shows, and retrospectives occurring in Santa Fe that weekend.

She checked her watch: nearly half past nine. Surely she had time to get out of the hotel and into town before Phillip began nosing around or before Pablo came down for breakfast and made things even more awkward. She signed the guest check and walked out to the valet's kiosk.

He shook his head. "Shuttle left half an hour ago, won't be back for forty-five minutes."

"Look, I'd like to be in town when…"

He grinned. "I can take you in my car, if you can wait 'til my break. Five minutes?"

She glanced at her watch again. "Sure, five minutes. That'll be fine."

Five minutes later, a luminescent blue—or was it purple?—Lincoln Town Car-turned-lowrider slid into view. The valet jumped out of the driver's seat to hold the door for her. Wynn lowered herself into the passenger seat. The valet climbed once more into the driver's side, kissed an index finger to the Virgin Mary on the dashboard, and pulled slowly away.

As they rolled down the mountain road, barely reaching the speed limit, she checked out the car's trappings: silver button-tufted door panels and matching upholstery, gray plush carpeting. "Nice ride," she said. "Nicer than the shuttle, I'm sure."

The valet flashed a smile. "Like it? See, lowriders aren't just cars, *qué no?*" His expression became earnest, eager. "The car says something about its owner, who he is, how he feels. This one is me. Me." He thumped his chest with two fingers. "I bought it from the hotel when they upgraded the rental car fleet. Took me three years to get it the way I wanted."

"The paint is…"

"Called Blue Velvet. The flecks of purple metallic give it a nice sheen, don't they?"

"Quite an undertaking."

"Yeah. I had the upholstery done special. But I did the hydraulics in the trunk myself. Great sound system, too." He pressed a button, and instantly the deafening trumpets of a salsa band blared from the front speakers as a thundering bass pounded from the back seat. "New Monster Cable."

Wynn nodded. The man might as well have been speaking in tongues, but he was taking her where she needed to go, and she appreciated that. She wanted to understand this car as well. It felt for all the world like a new art form.

"*Bajito y suavecito*, that's how we roll. Low and slow. So everyone can see and be amazed."

Wynn laughed, amazed by the automobile artist and his work of art.

"You want to go shopping?" he asked.

She shook her head. "The Canyon Road galleries. I heard about a *santero* from around here—I want to see his work."

"Many wonderful *santeros* around here, *señora*. The more holy the *santero*, the more powerful his artwork. Who is this *santero* you hear of?"

"His name is Ignacio Garza."

The car slowed.

He let her out at the entrance to Santa Fe's tree-lined Canyon Road, and she strolled along the famous walkway, pausing now and then to browse a gallery. Even in the first few blocks, there seemed no end to the variety of artwork on display: watercolors, photos of wild animals, wire sculptures,

CHAPTER TWELVE

computer-created works, and bizarre items made from found objects. It wasn't until she reached the point where Canyon Road crosses Delgado Street that she found what she was looking for: two galleries that specialized in Southwestern religious art—ancient, antique, and modern.

The first gallery, an ample white space highlighted by a beamed ceiling, featured antique *bulto* statues as well as century-old *retablos* painted on flat wood. Wynn enjoyed a comfortable familiarity with these, both from her studies and her work with Seamus Caine. She asked the woman behind the desk about three *santos* housed in a locked vitrine. The woman launched into the significance of them, but as she spoke, Wynn frowned. What were those *bultos* on the shelf behind the woman? Could they be from the same workshop as the ones in the hotel gift shop? She pointed, interrupting the history lesson, which promised to last until early afternoon, unimpeded. "And what can you tell me about those?"

The woman looked over her large black-rimmed glasses. "Oh. I thought you were only interested in the older ones."

"It's my field of expertise. But I heard about a *santero* named Ignacio Garza."

The woman arched an eyebrow and pointed toward the door. "*We* carry the finer work—dating to nineteen-forty-one. Across the street, *they* carry more"—she gave a disdainful sniff and pointed again toward the door—"… more commercial things. *He* may be able to help you over there."

Across the street, a young man scratched at his spiked blonde hair. "I've heard of Garza," he said. "But I'm beginning to think he's an urban legend. I don't know that I've ever seen any of his work. Much of the really good *santeros'* stuff is hard to find. They carve only for their village churches. They never sell it. Try up on Museum Hill," he said. "At the Folk Art Museum."

Wynn frowned and cocked her head. She thought she knew what he meant, but this was one of those times when she struggled with her head. And then suddenly she knew—*knew*—that this was the museum that had bought Pablo's San Gabriel. "At…?"

"Museum of International Folk Art." He jotted an address on the back of a business card. "Tell them I sent you."

DAY OF THE DEAD

* * *

DaShaye Williams leaned back in his chair at the Cruz County jail and rubbed the center of his forehead with the knuckle of one thumb. The investigation of Alejandra Ramirez's death was going nowhere. The absence of clues annoyed him. Though he'd seen Alejandra last winter, flouncing around the LaFonda Hotel down in Santa Fe in a fur coat and diamonds, he couldn't prove she ever owned them, still owned them, or that they had been stolen as part of the crime.

From what he found out about Alejandra she didn't hook for drugs—quite the reverse. She'd been clean for the eight years he'd been in Cruz County, that much he knew. Cruz County wasn't big enough for a user or a dealer to escape notice, and Alejandra was never on the radar. Her only high was marijuana—and she handed out joints almost as party favors.

Nor did she work through a pimp. She hooked because she made a living doing it, and she'd built a clientele that stretched into odd corners of society and strange parts of the world. Still, even though she'd apparently been working the night she was killed, Williams had found no cash and no murder weapon. She'd probably known whoever the doer was because there was no sign of forced entry. Well, he guessed there was no sign of forced entry; it was hard to tell in all that mess.

The woman had no family, neighbors said. Her mother and brother had been killed in a car accident on their way home from Taos a number of years back. She'd moved away for a while but came back. Got pregnant a couple of times—a risk of the trade, he supposed—and left town each time, but she always returned alone. She had no friends other than Ordierno Feliz, who visited occasionally, usually in the afternoons. According to the neighbors, the two would sit out in front of Alejandra's little adobe and talk, and then Feliz would leave. She had no real boyfriend.

Williams wondered how a person could live like that, with no one to talk to, no one who seemed to care. From the looks of things, Alejandra had spent her days watching QVC and ordering, and watching and ordering. He'd found QVC packing slips and gewgaws in every cabinet and drawer

CHAPTER TWELVE

in the house. And as cluttered as the place had been, the wastebaskets were empty. That was peculiar.

So then who had done her in? An angry john? Another whore? Some new cult leader come down from Talpa to rid the world of sin?

He wanted to solve this one without help from Feliz, so that he could use the collar to campaign on, but time was running out. The election was in two weeks, and so far, he had nothing.

The receptionist at the Folk Art Museum had been unimpressed with Wynn's business card and her introduction from the young man at the gallery. She shrugged. "We cannot help you, Mrs. Cabot. The curator is in a meeting and will be most of the day." She smiled and handed the business card back to Wynn.

"Is there someone, anyone, who might talk to me about—"

"No, I'm sorry. They are all in the same meeting."

Wynn took a breath and nodded. She, like The Terminator, would be back.

The electronic chime sounded as Wynn entered the hotel gift shop shortly after eleven that morning. A middle-aged man stood behind the counter, shuffling through a pile of crumpled invoices and receipts.

Wynn lifted a *bulto* of San Lorenzo from a shelf and studied it closely. The sandstone work to finish it was clumsy; the paint garish. This figure wasn't so much carved as chopped from the wood. The saint hadn't been liberated in his earthly form, he'd barely escaped. She lifted down a second one—a Saint Jude, waves of flame radiating from his head. The paint work was elegant, subtle. A matte burgundy patina in the crevasses gave it a glow unlike the others.

She glanced over her shoulder; the man behind the counter dusted and cleaned the glass on a display case, making a point, she thought, of ignoring her. Carrying both the crude *bulto* and the better one, she stepped to the cash register and gave a delicate cough.

Grudgingly, the shopkeeper laid down his cleaning supplies and looked at her, but said nothing.

"I wonder...," she said. "I'm curious about your *santos*. Where do they come from? Are they made around here?"

The man glanced at what she held. His face twisted in a mirthless smile. "Here in the Southwest we call those *bultos*."

"I know, but the whole—"

"This one—" he interrupted, snatching the carving from her hand and glancing at its base—"this *bulto* is made in a town called Arco Viejo. But, if you think to go there so you will not have to pay the price we charge here at Vista Cielo—"

"Oh, no..." Wynn waved a hand, hoping to smooth over any misunderstanding. So many times, she knew, tourists tried to buy direct from the artisans rather than pay the profit gift shops tacked on. She held out the Saint Jude. "Please, how much is this?"

The shopkeeper rolled his eyes and sighed. "I'll have to check." He tipped the figure to its bottom. His upper lip twitched. "Ah. This one is made by one of our best *escultors*—an old man named Ignacio Garza."

Wynn stifled a gasp.

"He lives in Arco Viejo," the shopkeeper continued. "The county seat of Cruz County—about an hour's drive from here. Over here, we have some more of Garza's work."

He led her back to the display of *santos*. Twelve *bultos* stood like apostles on a shelf, ranging in size from eight inches to two feet, in price from just under a hundred dollars to more than a thousand, and in quality from dross to reasonably good.

"All of these are by Ignacio Garza?"

The man paused, looking at her for several moments.

Wynn ignored his silence and continued to examine the *bultos* he had handed her, and then glanced at the man's face, noticing a subtle scar running from the edge of his right nostril across his cheek to the bottom of his right ear lobe. Odd, she thought. *Strange that I should be noticing scars as often as I am these days. What does that say about my state of mind, I wonder.*

He collected himself. "Sorry, I was thinking. Right. About half of them are made by Garza. This one"—he plucked a foot-tall figure, an exquisite San

CHAPTER TWELVE

Juan Bautista, from an upper shelf—"and this one, and this." He grabbed two mediocre pieces. "And these." He pushed the carvings forward.

"You're sure?"

"I beg your pardon?"

"It's just that—well, the quality is so obviously different from piece to piece." She took the crude San Juan Nepomuceno and held it next to the Saint Jude. "See? This one is smooth, the fingers are long and tapered, the paint is plain and matte. This one is rough, coarse—it's the same saint, in the same position, but the fingers are all clumped together. And the paint looks like it belongs on a lowrider."

"But I'm sure they are both by Ignacio Garza. He must have made this one many years ago… Perhaps his eyesight fades, and he cannot…"

Wynn gave a wry chuckle. "I'm sure you're right." She pursed her lips and frowned, then once again handed the Saint Jude to the shopkeeper. "I'll take this one, please."

He nodded, and she waited to speak until after she'd signed a room charge of four hundred dollars. "Now that I've proven I'm not trying to pull a fast one, can you tell me how to get to Arco Viejo?"

He shook his head. "I would feel bad directing you to the place." He shook a bony finger in her face. "And never think to drive to Arco Viejo alone," he said, wrapping the *bulto* in tissue and placing it in a box. "At this time of year, the weather can turn very fast. There may be other problems out there, too, but that road is *muy peligroso*."

"I'll bet it is," she said, gathering up her purchase and heading for the door. "But where would the adventure be if it weren't dangerous to somebody?"

Eliu Colón watched the comings and goings in the hotel lobby with a particularly keen eye, sensing, as he usually did at this time of year, a restlessness. Occupancy at the hotel had fallen off to barely fifty percent—unusually low for this time of year. And alcohol profits were down. Those who were in-house weren't drinking much. Something was wrong.

In a month, the hotel would be hosting ski bums who drank cheap beer and forty-rod scotch and got birthday drunk and tore up the rooms. He didn't know whether that was preferable to this free-floating agitation that had overtaken Vista Cielo, but to him, it seemed the archangels had already taken away the euphoria of summer. It felt as though he should guard his flanks.

The gift shop door shut noiselessly behind Wynn. Through the window, the salesman watched her cross the lobby. He'd been annoyed that he could not say more about the *bultos*, leaving her with the impression he didn't know much about what he sold. It was not his doing—*Señor* Colón's instructions had been that he shouldn't talk to anyone about the *bultos*. Clearly, the woman knew her stuff.

He pulled another *bulto* from the shelf and inspected it, then took down another, one that had been in the stock for a while, and compared the two. His hands trembled as he placed the two carvings back on the shelf at opposite ends, so that their contrasts would not be so obvious to the untrained eye. How had he missed it before? Or had he not wanted to believe it until this woman lectured him on the contradictions? Looking closely, the difference was obvious. He dusted paint flakes from his hands, allowed himself a moment of triumph, and then reached for his cell phone, punching in seven numbers.

"Yes. It's me," he said and took a deep breath. "I had a visitor today asking about our *bultos*." His mouth dried from the excitement, his hand shook. He paused to sip at his coffee.

"Go on," a soft voice on the other end prompted.

"A woman came in just now. A woman who knows about *santos*—knows as much as any of us do, maybe more. *Señor* Colón told me not to say anything about the *santos* unless I was asked a direct question, and then to give only the briefest of answers."

"And of course you did."

He sipped again at his coffee, letting the man on the other end wait. Then, "I did a lot of shrugging and claimed to know nothing."

"You were right to do that."

"But then, you see, I began to compare the *bultos* myself." Again he paused.

CHAPTER TWELVE

"It turns out I am not the idiot you expected me to be."

Now the voice on the other end paused briefly. "Oh, no?"

"I think I have found out your secret. My silence will cost more than the small change you pay me. Shall we say, twice as much?"

Neron Diaz had slept soundly the previous night. He always slept well when he stayed at Vista Cielo, partly because of the beds, all soft and clean and white, and partly because of the good meals that someone else made for him and brought to him to eat at a nice table with a clean white tablecloth on it. He slept well because of the amount of mescal and Pacifico he drank at the bar downstairs, and mostly he slept well because he didn't have to cut his sack time short to deal with the petty problems that seemed to crop up early every day out in Arco Viejo.

For some reason, El Eché had given him that pathetic town as a territory. Eché thought the Arco Viejo project was important, that *pequeña ciudad patética*. Pah. Important. What was important about a bunch of no-talent woodcarvers who lived to torment him, Nerón Diaz, the only cartel member ever to be deported back to the U.S. by the Mexican government?

He dreamed of a life where he could live full-time at places like Vista Cielo, not just when he had a job to do. He tried to think of a way to drag this trip out over several days, but perhaps El Eché would permit him to stay at Vista Cielo past tonight when he saw the results Diaz could produce. Later, he thought, he'd have a few drinks in the bar and a decent meal. And then a few more drinks before he returned to the beautiful white bed, and maybe not alone.

He had wakened just after two PM when El Eché called, and dressed and headed for the gift shop. No one threatened El Eché with extortion. Slipping on his gloves, he pushed into the shop.

Fifteen minutes later, Diaz found Eliu Colón at the front desk. His face said nothing; he merely relayed with a nod and a jerk of a thumb across his neck that a dead man lay in the gift shop.

Colón's eyes narrowed, and he clenched his bulldog jaw. *"Idiota,"* he rasped.

Diaz flapped his arms in mid-air. "It wasn't me—I swear," he said. "He was dead when I walked in." He shrugged, his hands supplicant. "Whoever did it made a mess. Not the way I would have done it. Not the way I would have done it at all."

He couldn't afford to be arrested again. He'd been out nearly three years, and though he'd made good money in prison, he'd never made the kind of money he was making now. He longed to be back in Mexico with the cartel, where he belonged. If he made enough money on this damned Arco Viejo project, he could spend the rest of his days drinking *pulche* in Veracruz while he pleasured a host of beautiful *señoritas*.

Colón stared at him for a long moment, and then glanced over the man's bald head, seeing movement at the gift shop door. A woman had entered. He shoved Diaz aside and, with a flick of his head, said, "Go," and then he turned back to his work and waited for the inevitable scream.

Chapter Thirteen

A phalanx of white patrol cars pulled under the *porte-cochère* and up to the entrance of Vista Cielo. Ordierno Feliz got out of the lead car and sniffed. The late afternoon had cooled, and he smelled piñon smoke drifting from the kiva fireplaces in the hotel's better guest rooms.

The valet appeared at his elbow. "Leave it right where it is," Feliz snapped.

Inside, guests and hotel staff collected at the lobby entrance craning their necks to see what went on.

For the second time in two days, Feliz bent down to inspect a corpse lying at his feet. The victim was face down on the floor in front of the shelf of *bultos*, spread-eagled in a pool of blood. His body appeared untouched until Feliz lifted his head, took note of the hole in the man's skull, the broken eye socket exposing bare bone where the skin had peeled away, and an old scar stretching from the victim's right nostril to his right ear lobe. He gulped back a wave of nausea brought on by the smell of blood.

He glanced over his shoulder to see Eliu Colón fawning over a couple who seemed concerned that a dead man lay in the hotel gift shop. The murder had occurred during the peak traffic hours through the lobby, and it was Colón's job to pacify his guests.

Ordinarily, Feliz liked Vista Cielo. The place was on the outer edge of Cruz County—even though the hotel claimed it was in Santa Fe, it sat just over the county line—a fair drive from Santa Fe's plaza. Felix used the hotel whenever he wanted to unwind or entertain. People on his Important Donor List—judges, legislators, and the governor—frequented Vista Cielo as dinner patrons and came and went relatively anonymously as overnight guests.

Some recent changes to the area made Feliz nervous, though. Developers from Texas and California had brought in the recent rash of spas with their hot rock massages and chakra pools and the stupid jeep tours that had birding tourists running all over Cruz County, pointing and climbing and needing to be rescued from places they should never have been in the first place. Why didn't they confine themselves to prettying up hotels and churches in Mexico and Canada rather than bothering his little corner of heaven?

The people of New Mexico had endured long before the rest of the U.S. decided that New Mexico's poverty and corruption could be helped by chakra pools and bird-watching safaris, and hundred-dollar dinners. When New Mexico held a mirror up to the rest of America, people turned away, afraid of the terrible beauty that drugs and violence could shape.

Eliu Colón separated himself from the woman who had found the body and stood motionless, in a sort of mute hysteria, in the doorway to the gift shop; he was the rock, as he liked to think of himself, the rock in the stream with the current flowing around him. He interrupted his reverie and spread his arms in greeting. "Sheriff Feliz, you came quickly."

Feliz smiled up at him and then nodded in the direction of the victim. "This sucks."

Colón nodded. "This could be a public relations disaster for Vista Cielo. Try to be discreet, *por favor*. The guests—we must not let any more of them know of this tragedy."

"Nobody saw anything?"

"Of course not."

"Who found him?"

Colón flipped a thumb in the direction of the overwrought woman and sneered. "I'm afraid we will have to give her a free night or two in exchange for her…uh…trauma."

Feliz pulled a clean white handkerchief from his pocket to wipe blood off his hands. "*Señor* Colón," Feliz called. "Is there money in the till?"

Colón shook his head.

Feliz nodded. "You were the first to check that the man was dead?"

CHAPTER THIRTEEN

Colón's nostrils flared. "He would not want to live, knowing he had been robbed."

"So we may assume robbery." Feliz stood. "This is officially a crime scene. Let's treat it like one." He caught movement to his right and glanced over, seeing the coroner shuffle in, clad in protective paper shoes, gown and cap. "Oh, Mr. Jackson, how nice of you to dress for the occasion."

Jackson knelt and opened his bag, but said nothing to Feliz. The sheriff's disdain for a crime scene made working it more difficult, and Jackson had quietly contributed in whatever way he could to see that Feliz lost the upcoming election.

Feliz stood over the ME. "The victim obviously died of blunt force trauma to the head, wouldn't you say? Your services aren't needed, are they? If you have somewhere else to be?"

"I have all day, Feliz, and nowhere to be other than here. We may be able to learn something more from this one than the last." He held out an arm, pushing Feliz away. "Give me room."

DaShaye Williams set his fingerprint case on the counter. "While he's doing that, I can dust for prints."

"For God's sake," Colón whined. "It's a hotel gift shop. It'll have the fingerprints of every guest who's been in here in the past year."

Williams looked from Colón to Feliz, bewilderment in his eyes. "All right then." Williams capped a vial of fingerprint dust and put away his brushes. "But we'll want to question everyone—guests, staff, vendors, the whole shebang."

"Do you have to do that?" Colón moaned. "It'll disrupt everything. They'll resent your insinuendoes."

Williams frowned. "Insinu…" Sometimes his knowledge of Spanish lagged, but this word, this one he had never… "Wait. We aren't questioning them as suspects. It's just that they might have seen something."

"Even if—"

Feliz pulled Williams and Colón to the door. "Guys, we seem to be at a dead end. Officer Williams, you are free to interview staff, but guests are off-limits. Colón, put a flyer in the rooms asking the guests to call the police if they've seen anything—"

"And assuring them that their tips will remain anonymous," Colón prompted.

"Of course. But this shop will remain closed and taped."

Colón spread his hands, supplicant. "Does the gift shop have to be taped? Think what that will look like—just off the lobby. And closed? It's a major source of income for the hotel. I need to have it open to make the kind of money that— That some people expect it to make."

DaShaye Williams raised his voice a notch. "It's a crime scene until we have everything we need."

The coroner spoke without looking up. "By the way, the tests came back on Alejandra Ramirez already. Apparently things are slow in Albuquerque today, too."

Feliz waited. "And? Do we have to guess what they said?"

"Tox screen showed point-one-oh for whiskey, but no drugs," Jackson said. "And I found ligature marks on her wrists. I'm thinking probably she was tied to the bedposts at some point."

DaShaye Williams nodded. "No money at Alejandra's place—none that I found, anyway, and I looked pretty thoroughly. Odd for a woman who runs a cash business, don't you think? No money and her mink coat and jewelry were gone—I'd seen her in that coat. It was a nice one." He flipped his notebook closed. "The only rental car agency that has a black Cadillac Escalade like the one seen leaving Alejandra's place is right here at the hotel. A guy named Phillip Cabot, a guest, took it out that night." He gestured toward the front counter of the gift shop. "And you say the cash register here has been cleaned out, too."

Feliz wanted to be somewhere else right now—anywhere else. So Williams had looked for money at Alejandra's place after Feliz left but found none. Well, yes, that was right. But the coat? Her jewelry? Who the hell had taken those?

"This goes deeper than a simple robbery, I think." He flashed his cuffs, noticing a spatter of red on one, and looked at his gold Cartier watch. He had a fundraiser later, dammit; he couldn't spend time screwing around here.

CHAPTER THIRTEEN

* * *

As the sun set, a chilly late-October evening moved in. Feliz leaned back in his chair in the hotel dining room and watched a young woman hang a garland of brightly colored paper flowers around the hostess's podium.

Ah, yes, he thought, Halloween. He really hoped there would be none of the usual bullshit stunts this year. "Please, Jesus, let this one be manageable," he muttered. There were already enough skeletons around as Day of the Dead décor. He didn't need to hear about driverless cars ordering Happy Meals at McDonald's or dismembered fingers in the middle of a pizza out at Domino's.

He reached over and opened a nearby patio door a few inches to let some air into the room, knowing it would be fragrant with the earthy smell of piñon smoke and the promise of winter. Weather forecasters called for a cold front and snow late next week. Tonight would be a good night for *caldos*. The restaurant's mouth-searing red chile soup reminded him of home.

Home. For years, while he grew up, home had been the parish house in Arco Viejo. His mother had left him with the priest, Father Hernandez, when he was four, promising to return in a year or so, after she got clean in El Paso. She'd never come back. He'd grown up in Arco Viejo, peddling grass and cocaine out of the parish house, and fighting almost continually with the other boy the *padré* had struggled to raise—the nasty piece of work named Nerón Diaz.

Then came the day that Feliz rescued seven-year-old Eliu Colón from drowning in the quarry pond, and he realized that he could be someone his community respected, and that he might one day deserve the love of Lisa Guzman.

Feliz relived that day: Carrying the bleeding boy in his arms, he staggered into Arco Viejo, onlookers staring as he walked to the plaza and laid the child on the *banco* that surrounded the fountain.

No one gave any thought to how the boy's blood stains might leave marks on the adobe bench—tell-tale tracks from the lateral gashes in his back and the backs of his arms. Until rain and snow erased the smears from the *banco* in the months to come, those would be evidence of Eliu Colón's beating and Feliz's heroism—a tale that would flourish for a few days and then fade with the end of summer, replaced with the harvest festivals, Christmas galas, and next spring's passion play.

Indeed, Arco Viejo relied on the natural order of things—their feast days and the seasons, *penitentés* and politicians, and the village's tradition of *santeros*, artisans who carved the iconic wood images of saints. The people lived by these rhythms and rituals, had for centuries, and they saw no reason to change.

Sometimes it was necessary, they thought, for a man to correct his children in ways the outside world might think severe. After Feliz brought Eliu back into town on that late September day, there had been whispers that the boy's father had taken him to the abandoned limestone quarry to "teach him to swim," but there had been no outrage at the severity of the boy's punishment. Of course, they said, the elder Colón hadn't meant for the boy to tangle a foot in the roots of the willows that grew along the water's edge.

Feliz had been close by, near the old mine shaft, harvesting marijuana plants he'd grown there when he heard the kid call out. He'd climbed the hill to the top and saw the elder Colón—a knuckle-bone-cruel man—coiling a short whip in his hand and walking away, leaving his son to struggle in the morass of tree roots in the pond at the foot of the rock face.

Feliz knew he shouldn't intervene. What a father did to punish his son was his own business, but this was rattlesnake mean. He waited until Colón was out of sight, then scrabbled down the slope, hoping Colón wouldn't hear the splash when he dived into the quarry pond. He surfaced underneath the boy, grabbed him up by his armpits and pulled him free of the tree roots. He hadn't realized the boy was bleeding so profusely until the kid rolled away from him on the grass to cough up water.

Feliz carried the boy more than three miles to town, and oh, what adulation the villagers heaped upon him when they realized he had rescued little Eliu Colón, the barber's son, from drowning. Their praise gave Feliz a confidence he'd never known until that day—a sense of fearlessness, of being invincible,

CHAPTER THIRTEEN

the kick-start Feliz needed to contemplate greater things than to spend his life selling weed or stuccoing adobes alongside the *ancianas*.

Some in town, though, were privately annoyed with Feliz's newfound favor. Why, the nerve of the seventeen-year-old, daring to call the mayor by his first name—and who was Ordierno Feliz to ask Lisa Guzman, the banker's daughter, to go down to Santa Fe with him to see *Indecent Proposal*?

Naturally, Lisa's father had insisted they stay put—and in plain sight—rather than go as far afield as Santa Fe, and so, accompanied by the inevitable Eliu, the young couple went for walks along the jagged cut of the Rio Grande gorge on Sunday afternoons. Though Colón was younger than the teenaged Feliz by ten years, as he recovered from his gashes and near drowning in the quarry pond, he became Feliz's *segundo al mando*, his campaign manager, his shadow. At seven, Eliu's memory was as short as he was, and in a month or so he had nearly forgotten exactly why he felt such a strong bond with his *hermano*, thinking only that being in the company of the older boy was normal—sure that Feliz had been destined to be his *patrono*, a partnership that would last from that golden autumn until this one, twenty years later.

Feliz inhaled deeply. Some of his life had gone right after that—he'd found his calling in law enforcement—but that thing with Lisa…that thing with Lisa. Between chasing around raising funds for his re-election and trying to do his job, life was becoming a real nuisance. Were it not for all the side benefits he'd cultivated over the past years as sheriff, he would happily flip his badge to DaShaye Williams and go back to dealing drugs.

As for finding out who drove the black Cadillac Escalade the night Alejandra was killed, he'd found that, more often than not, questioning a person of interest was a waste of time. An invitation to skip town. A dead-end that might result in bad publicity and threats of lawsuits. If he played it right, the murderer would show himself without Feliz having to lift a finger. He would wait another day or so—a suitable suspect would turn up.

Phillip's dinner invitation left Wynn feeling vaguely guilty. Had someone on the hotel staff told him about her previous visits here with Pablo? Why hadn't she left the hotel the minute Phillip showed up? Why had she come here at all?

The two of them met in the lobby, picked their way through the tangle of sheriff's deputies and police paraphernalia, and walked on to the dining room. Without a word to each other or to the hostess, they slid into a banquette adjacent to Feliz's table. With a flourish, the hostess spread napkins on their laps.

The gleaming tableware, the warmth and aroma of the fireplace, the cheerful paper-flower garlands draped throughout the room—none of it helped lighten Wynn's mood. She stared at her empty water glass until water being splashed into it startled her.

"Good evening," a waiter chirped. "My name is Jorgé, and I'll be your server this evening. May I start you off with a cocktail? Perhaps a glass of wi—"

"Gentleman Jack. Double. And tell the bartender *Señor* Cabot is in the restaurant. He knows how to pour my Jack."

Wynn frowned. "Is a drink right now a good—"

"God damn it." He threw his napkin on his plate. "I'll have a drink if I want to."

Wynn lowered her gaze to the tabletop once more, thinking. Phillip hadn't been like this when they first married—but more and more, she forgot how love felt. When she and Phillip were married, she'd felt as if the party had just begun. Wanted to crawl inside his skin to be closer to him.

She could tell her husband was on edge, straining at the leash, eager for… something.

She glanced at him, hearing again the marriage counselor's words when Phillip hadn't shown up for yet another session: "Nothing you do or say will make him come. He has to want to be part of this relationship; it must come from him. Dare him to leave. If he stays willingly, then he loves you in whatever way it is that he knows how to love—and I'm warning you that may be a stunted kind of affection, Wynn. But if he leaves…"

It's up to you, she thought. *Do you really want to be here with me? Because I can't*

CHAPTER THIRTEEN

make you stay unless you want to.

Cabot took her hand but looked away. Almost whispering, he said, "It gets hard sometimes, Wynn. I need…"

"What, Phillip?" she said. "Tell me."

"More. I need more." He looked at her, his jaw set. "This life owes me—the best job, more money, hell, even the best golf score."

"You didn't used to—"

"I know, but these days I'm not happy unless I'm riding the biggest Harley or building a better shopping mall or…drinking whiskey that's more expensive than the last stuff I had. The older I get, the more I need. And every minute I'm not getting the biggest and the best and the most expensive…I feel like I'm backsliding. It's this constant drive I have, but all the same, it's what keeps me going." He shook his head as though he didn't understand it himself. "You're a good woman—the most beautiful, capable, kind woman I've ever met. And I need that woman always, the best woman I can ever find."

He straightened and took his ringing cell phone from his jacket pocket, glancing at its face. "This is Tripp. I have to take it." He turned his back to her and mumbled into the phone.

His confession explained a lot, Wynn thought, but it excused nothing—not his philandering, or the drug use, or the drinking. He sounded so earnest, but she couldn't get a read on him anymore. Until the phone rang, everything he said and all his body language told her he wanted to be here with her tonight. And then…

"Let me know," Cabot said into the phone, turning back to the table. "Let me know, you know, when…" He ended the call and shook his head, then glanced at her, conscious of her stare. "What?" he asked.

"The minute a conversation gets meaningful, you take a phone call."

"I can't choose when a call from my attorney comes in, you know. What'd I just tell you? I married you because you're more woman than—"

"Maybe I'm more woman… but apparently I'm not *enough* woman. Cut the charade and go home."

At the next table, Feliz cleared his throat and called for Jorgé.

Cabot lowered his head and his voice. "I can't."

55

"What do you mean, you can't?"

"I can't go home. Tripp says I have to…stay gone for a while."

"You're joking."

He shook his head. "The city's taking bids on that new convention complex. But the fact is I've already got the contract."

"How?"

He grinned. "I went directly to the guy responsible for the project. While those dumb bastards in City Procurement are leading fools through the bid process, I'm already signed and sealed."

"Then why can't you go home?"

"Because one of the dumbass bidders got wind of it and went to the press. The city attorney is looking for me, and I'm out of the state for an unspecified period, spending time with my family."

Wynn was out of the banquette in two moves. "I'm not hungry." She fled the room in swift strides.

"…the fuck?" he called after her. "You play by the rules, you lose." He watched her go, then shrugged.

Feliz raised his glass to Cabot. "She is quite a woman, that one," he said. "And easily aroused in other ways, no?"

Cabot motioned to Jorge for another drink and glared at Feliz. "Mind your own fucking business."

Knowing there would be no dinner tab, Feliz rose from the table and left the restaurant. Cabot watched Feliz's back, loathing the way the man rolled his feet in his smarmy soft-leather loafers, disgusted by the fey raw silk sport coat he wore. Cabot stared down into his Jack neat.

"Do you want to order now?" Jorgé asked. "Or will you wait for the lady?"

"The lady isn't coming back," Cabot said. "And I'm not hungry yet. Bring me another double."

Ordierno Feliz crossed the hotel lobby to the gift shop and stopped, rocking back on his heels while he watched DaShaye Williams work. "How's it going?"

Williams scratched his chin in a move Feliz thought made the deputy look more squirrely than thoughtful. "I'll be here a while."

CHAPTER THIRTEEN

Feliz nodded and checked his watch. He needed to get to his fundraiser. "You got it under control. I'm going to take off." Good old, by-the-book Williams would drag out these murder investigations, both Alejandra's and now this one, for months if he could. That was fine with Feliz. Perhaps he would call a press conference. As long as he could say the cases were ongoing, even past the election—especially past the election—the public would be happy.

Chapter Fourteen

The following morning Phillip Cabot drowned his hangover in blue corn pancakes and then went to the spa to sweat out the remains of last night's Gentleman Jack. He showered, dressed in a windshirt, tour pants, and Footjoys, and phoned the valet desk to have the black Escalade brought around front.

Special Agent André Bishop had talked to Seamus Caine earlier—at three-thirty in the morning, for Chrissakes—and got the lowdown on Wynn Cabot's maladjustment. Her head misfired, Caine explained—that must have been what was going on when she squinted at the Sotheby's catalog sheets the previous evening.

At ten, Bishop pulled his government-issue Ford sedan under the *porte-cochère* at Vista Cielo to wait for the Cabot woman. The two of them were going out to Arco Viejo to see if they could shake loose any information from the *santeros*. He pulled a file folder from his briefcase and checked the enlargements of the catalog sheets he'd made at Caine's suggestion.

"She isn't stupid, dear boy," Caine had said. "Far from it. So watch yourself."

Fair enough, Bishop thought. He liked smart women, liked to be around them—especially smart, pretty women—but so far, they didn't seem to care much for him. He'd bought books on how to be popular, books that always said the same things: make eye contact, smile, be a good listener, shower daily, and use deodorant. All of that failed once he was required to open his mouth, because as much as he knew about art, everything he knew about talking to women would fit in a thimble.

CHAPTER FOURTEEN

He'd even studied some of the other agents—their cool moves, their confidence, the way they dressed and buffed up. Nothing worked. He'd been single his entire life, try as he might to attract the kinds of women he thought he could spend time with.

He withdrew his phone from his pocket and dialed the number for Alejandra Ramirez. Nothing, yet again. Nothing but dead silence.

A metal-flake gold Corvette pulled through the *porte-cochère*, and the driver, a bald guy in a wife-beater, backed the car into a nearby parking place. The valet pulled a black Cadillac Escalade alongside the government-issue Ford and hoisted a fully-loaded, expensive-looking golf bag into the back.

Out of the corner of his eye Bishop saw the hotel's front doors open and Wynn Cabot step out onto the paved driveway. Bishop hurried to hold the passenger door for her and heard, over his shoulder, a man's voice shout, "Where the fuck do you think you're going, and who's this asshole?"

Wynn got out of the Ford and walked around Bishop to face the man behind him. "To Arco Viejo with …" She gestured in Bishop's direction.

Bishop nodded to Cabot.

Cabot snatched at her arm, but missed. The hangover had affected his reflexes. "Don't walk away from me. I caught you leaving with a cheap suit, is that right?"

Wynn sighed. "Phillip, this is Special Agent André Bishop—from the FBI. Agent Bishop, this is my husband. We're not getting along at the moment, as you can no doubt tell."

"Let's see some ID, Agent Bishop."

Bishop pulled his leather ID folder from the breast pocket of his sport coat and flipped it open, making sure, as he replaced it, that he revealed the straps of his shoulder holster.

Cabot stepped back, first one step, and then three before he turned and called over his shoulder, "Well, you two have a nice day. I have a tee time." He waved and disappeared into the waiting Escalade.

They rode in silence out past run-down mobile homes that dotted the edge of town, past a deserted diner and a monument company that displayed out front a number of marble headstones resting at odd angles, blank where names would one day be etched. A large, intricately carved angel prayed over the dusty yard.

Wynn flipped through the enlargements of the Sotheby's catalog pages, reading the descriptions, comparing the auction-house hammer prices, studying the photographs of each piece while she thought. The encounter with Phillip had been unsettling, but of course, he'd backed off when faced with an FBI agent.

Even so, she wished she hadn't come this morning; the only question she and Bishop had for the *santeros* was nothing more than a veiled accusation—why were they creating duplicates of a statue that had disappeared one hundred and fifty years ago and selling each of them as the original? And was Ignacio Garza one man or a group of *santeros* working under one name—as sometimes occurred? Did he even exist at all?

Bishop's questions had more to do with the woman in the passenger seat: Okay, so her head misfired—had that played a part in picking a consummate asshole for a husband? And if he was as abusive as he seemed, why did she stay with him? Was the guy dangerous, or was he all mouth and no trousers?

They both spoke at once.

"How long have you—" Bishop began.

"The *san*—" Wynn said. She sat back. "Go ahead. How long have I...what?"

"I was wondering how long you and The Mister have been married. None of my business, really. Just wondering."

"Right. It isn't your business. Five years. But we haven't lived together for the past year."

"Oh. Aha. He seems to think you're still—"

"He followed me here without my knowing about it. I don't know how much more clearly I can say it to him. When I moved out, I told him I wasn't staying in the relationship any longer. He didn't want to hear it. He thinks it's time for me to move back home. Well, it's not home, not for me—but move back *in* with him."

Bishop said nothing for a time and then, "What did you start to say?"

"Oh. Well, the *santeros*, they have to know it's just a matter of time before

CHAPTER FOURTEEN

someone—namely, you and I—go out there and start nosing around, wouldn't you think?"

Cottonwood trees arched overhead. Bright crepe paper streamers wafted in the late morning breeze; smiling *papier maché* skulls gazed from adobe walls and grinned from windows. Billows of gold marigolds spilled from baskets and planters, and *serapé*-draped altars to the recently-deceased rested in front yards. In the center of the plaza, men piled miscellaneous pieces of wood, preparing a Halloween bonfire. Arco Viejo's decorating for The Day of the Dead had begun.

Bishop parked his Ford sedan in front of the grocery store. An old priest rose from his spot on the *banco* that surrounded the fountain and walked slowly toward the car, leaning down to look in the driver's window.

"A spirit guide, no doubt," Wynn said.

Bishop nodded. "Looks like." He rolled down the window. "Hi there, *Padré*. You have some fine *santeros* around here, no?"

"Smooth," Wynn mumbled.

The priest said nothing but did not move from his position, his gaze still fixed on the two of them. Bishop rolled up the window, opened the car door and stood, shielding himself with the door.

The priest reached into his front pants pocket and removed a short metal shaft with a rosewood inset, pressed the button, and a long stiletto blade snapped into his open palm. He held his hand out, exhibiting the piece to Bishop, and then slowly closed his fingers around the knife's hasp. He held it up to Bishop's face, clutching it until his knuckles whitened.

Without a word, Bishop sat once again in the car and pulled the door closed.

Wynn frowned. "What was all that about?"

"Switchblade. I don't think I want to tangle with the *padré*. Didn't I read that his workshop is next to the river? Let's go down there and see what we can find."

Bishop fired up the Ford, backed away, and then circled outside the town until he found a rutted dirt road that led down a switch-back to the river. A low warehouse building, its doors open, sat at the bottom of the road. From inside came sounds of saws and hammers and sanding machines.

Ignacio Garza stood outside the workshop, talking in a tone barely audible over the sounds of machinery inside. "I was raised in a family of *santeros*," he said. "Worked in their studio, learning to carve the saints."

Wynn smiled. How pleased she was to finally meet the legendary *santero*—she couldn't fire questions fast enough. "Did you go to school?"

"Oh, *sí*, I graduated from the university in sixty-six, and then I got out of Albuquerque as fast as I could. It was too big. Too worldly. I came to Arco Viejo to work..." Garza's thought trailed off. He wiped his mouth with the back of a hand. "Arco Viejo was different then. More peaceful. A simple, small town."

Bishop watched the river below while he spoke. "You came to work on your carving?"

"Yes. In the late sixties, the town was quiet... quieter. I had time to research the lives of the saints. And to study the ways of the old *santeros*—things that kept me in touch with the spiritual aspects of my work. But Arco Viejo—"

Wynn felt starstruck, as though she had met a rock idol. "Your work is among the finest I've ever seen, *Señor* Garza."

The old man chuckled. "A long time since anyone has called me *Señor* Garza. Just Ignaz is fine. Please." He gestured toward the open doors of the warehouse. "There are some very fine young *santeros* working in there—they need to be..." He looked in and paused, lost in thought.

Wynn followed his stare, seeing younger men, and one woman, carving and painting. The colors they used were brighter than those Garza seemed to prefer. The young woman bent to embed jewels into the *bulto* in front of her, while a young man to her right sprinkled his *retablo* with mica and gold dust for sparkle.

"I've seen many of your pieces in the galleries and shops in Santa Fe. Do you do all the work yourself, or do the young *santeros* help?"

Garza shrugged. "You win an award or two, and you're on your way. I'm most proud of my *bultos* and *retablos* that are in the churches. The things in

CHAPTER FOURTEEN

the gift shops..." He laid a hand on Wynn's arm and looked at her, his eyes speaking something he couldn't say. He staggered a step. "The saints have not been as kind as I had hoped."

Wynn helped the old *santero* to a tree stump where he sat. "My father was killed a few years after I moved here, and for a while, I lost my faith. It took me many years to discover that the saints and angels have always been with me, but they do not dwell here in this place." He stared at the river, barely trickling below. "They are at my grandmother's house in Pilar... they are in my dreams. But they are not here."

Wynn turned away and frowned—this was getting awkward. It was time to get to the reason for their visit. "Do you know of the Zuni San Gabriel, *Señor* Garza?"

"Of course. Why do you ask?"

"Because it seems we—or rather Agent Bishop, here—his people... have seen it three times in the last year."

"No. No, they haven't." Garza shook his head wearily.

Bishop nodded. "Yes, they have. In London. In Zurich. And in New York. How would that be, I wonder?"

Again Garza shrugged. "A miracle, perhaps. Maybe San Gabriel returns to announce another holy birth. Who knows?"

"Or maybe the *bultos* are duplicates being sold as the original?"

Garza stood abruptly and stared past them. "Leave Arco Viejo," he said. "Go. We are not the town we were fifty years ago. The man behind you, standing at the top of the hill... his allegiance is no longer to God."

Chapter Fifteen

The rawboned, gray-haired man in a black cleric's shirt and pants was barely distinguishable from the angular shadows in the hotel hallway. His left hand carried a gym bag. His right hand checked his pants pocket, feeling the heft of his switchblade, and then he gasped. No—no! Not arrhythmia now. He'd been so healthy until recently. So strong. He hated giving into a weakness—any weakness—in his body. He gave three short taps on Pablo Estrella's door and then dragged a knuckle downward—his usual code.

Estrella opened the door and motioned the visitor inside.

The priest steadied himself with a hand to the wall and gasped for air. His heart thrummed in his throat. "Water, *por favor?*"

Quickly Estrella ran tap water into a plastic glass and wrapped the man's gnarled fingers around it. "I thought we might get a bite to eat."

The priest tossed the gym bag on the bed, removed a white pill from his pants pocket, slipped it between his lips, drank a sip of water, and then shook his head. "No. We'd be seen together." He moved into the room and sat on the edge of the bed, waiting for the effects of the tablet to quell the dizziness that always came with the stress of doing business. He felt strength return to his hands and arms, to his back, to his legs.

Estrella glanced out the balcony door, straining to see to his left and down toward the dining terrace. "It's after eight. There's nobody around in the dining room, and I'm hungry."

The man frowned at Estrella. "I said no. Let's see what you've brought me."

"Always right to business with you, isn't it? Here." Estrella pulled a *bulto*

CHAPTER FIFTEEN

from a high shelf in the small closet—a cottonwood *bulto* of San Lorenzo, slightly more than three feet tall, clad in a multicolored chasuble and stole. The figure reached forward, his hand curved as though he'd once held something.

The priest smiled and nodded. "Where did this one come from?"

"Tucson. The cathedral."

The priest moved to a lamp near the balcony door to study the statue's details. He tried not to gasp—it was faultless. He hadn't seen a San Lorenzo as masterfully done as this one since he'd first seen the *bulto* that originally took his breath away—the piece in the chapel at Truchas, on the high road to Taos, more than forty years ago.

The *santero* who had carved this one was, of course, legendary—all of the priest's *bultos* were bits of artisanal history—but this one was masterful, both inventive and touching. Fashioned out of a single piece of cottonwood, the figure's fingernails, the texture of the hair, the detail in the raiment, were all perfect. He could make out several layers of colored pigment under the brown top coat, a sign of the painstaking work to give the paint depth and richness.

The hunger to possess this piece at almost any price flared from his heart and spread throughout his body. "You paid the diocese decent money for this, I hope? Somewhere near what I told you to pay?"

Estrella did not answer.

"OK," the priest said, stronger now that both nitroglycerine and obsession coursed through his veins. "What did you pay?"

Still, Estrella said nothing.

"I asked you a question. How much did you pay for the *bulto*?"

"Enough."

"How much?" the priest demanded.

"I didn't pay anything, okay?"

"You stole it."

"Yeah." Estrella looked down at the pool, seeing Wynn Cabot sitting on the edge, dangling her feet in the water. He had lied to her—he still stole and forged and conned when he could. He wasn't proud of himself, but that was who he was. If she refused to be his salvation, then he couldn't be saved. He turned and faced the priest. "All you have to pay me for is my time. But since you're not paying for the *bulto*, my fee is double."

"Stealing wasn't the idea. We have enough gold to—"

"Oh, no? What's the difference? Maybe not so much."

"I buy these pieces legitimately."

"At a fraction of the cost."

The priest tapped the San Lorenzo on the palm of his free hand like a baton. "El Eché will not be happy that you stole from the church—any church. In addition to the *bulto*, I think you will need to tithe something, no? Shall we say, fifteen thousand dollars?"

"Impossible. That's all the money I have."

"Yes, I know. Coincidentally that's how much you got for the San Gabriel you sold to the Folk Art Museum yesterday—or so the newspaper article said."

"I'm not paying El Eché anything. You have your *bulto*. I have delivered that." Estrella crossed the room, reached for the gym bag, and unzipped it.

"Then I will tell Senator Guzman what you have been doing, *que no*? That you are using her?"

Estrella chuckled. "No, you won't. You won't say anything because El Eché doesn't need the FBI and the cops nosing around his collection, asking where the pieces came from."

With his free hand, the priest rubbed his face, stubbled with a gray beard. "You're a fool, Estrella." He snickered. "I think you maybe do not know what you are involved in. You do not refuse El Eché."

"Then I demand to see El Eché and not his errand boy." Estrella pushed the priest back toward the door, impressed by the man's power to resist.

"*Chingar!*" The priest swung the *bulto* hard, smashing it into Estrella's left ear.

Estrella reeled from the blow. Clutching his head, he staggered out onto the balcony, the older man hurtling out behind him. As Estrella straightened, holding up his arm to block the charge, the priest lunged but caught a foot on the door frame and fell forward. Estrella lowered and head-butted him in

CHAPTER FIFTEEN

the chest. The priest doubled. Estrella grasped his head and dug his thumbs into his eyes.

Blinded, the priest drove the *bulto* into Estrella's groin, pushing him away.

Estrella gasped but mustered the strength to stand just as the priest smashed the statue into his skull. The force of the blow drove Estrella's head and shoulders out over the balcony rail. And then, in slow motion, his balance tipped forward, his feet rose and followed his body down.

Chapter Sixteen

Standing at the edge of the dining terrace, Wynn Cabot gazed beyond the entry of the hotel's horseshoe shape on toward the stables and up to the actual vista cielo, the view of Heaven itself. To the west, beyond Santa Fe, the Sangre de Cristo Mountains fulfilled their name—at sunset, they were as red as the blood of Christ.

The sky darkened in a rainbow roll; the day's heat dissipated into the velvety blue New Mexican night sky—a sky the color of the valet's lowrider. Guests milled across the broad patio toward the dining room, leaving Wynn alone at the far end of the pool.

She knelt at the pool's edge, then kicked off her sandals and sat, trailing her feet in the cool water while she thought. She looked once again toward the lights of Santa Fe and the mountains beyond, the horizon banded in the last orange light of day. And then she frowned into the shadows—what was that noise? There it was again—thumps and growls from up above, on the far side of the building. She stood, and as she raised her gaze to the second-floor balconies, a body fell in front of her—a man, she thought—someone who did not reach to break his fall or cry out when his head struck the edge of the pool. Then the body tumbled into the aqua water, the momentum of the fall pushing the body, silhouetted black against the pool lights, down against the drain. Eddies of pink swirled from a head wound as blood streamed from the man's scalp.

Wynn ran to the deep end and dove in, knowing she had scant time before the air in the man's lungs was replaced by water. She grabbed hold of his shirt collar, broke the surface, glanced briefly at his face, then swam toward

CHAPTER SIXTEEN

the side of the pool, shaking, not from the wetness of her clothes in the cold night air, but from shock and fear. Near the raw wound on the man's head she had spotted what she knew this man called his angel kiss—the small, star-shaped birthmark near his hairline, the mark that matched his name, Estrella.

How many times had she stroked a lock of dark hair off his forehead and kissed the star before they parted, sometimes for only brief moments, sometimes for agonizing weeks, and each time she said, "*Adios, mi estrella.*"

And he would pull her close, smiling his soft, shiny-eyed smile. "*Tu es mi estrella. Mi madre* would have loved you as I love you."

"Not quite," she would giggle, kissing the star once more, her ginger-colored hair falling across his face. "Oh, not even close."

Now, hauling his body up the stairs at the shallow end of the pool, she laid him out on the red-tile terrace near the *al fresco* dining tables, grabbed a towel off a chaise longue to cushion his head, knelt and checked for a pulse at his neck.

And felt nothing.

Phillip Cabot crossed the parking lot and tossed the Escalade's keys to the valet. He stumbled on the pavement and caught himself before he fell. Maybe he shouldn't have had that last drink at the clubhouse, but damn, it had been a good day, and he felt like celebrating—he'd shot two over par and brought that course to its knees. He passed a metal-flake gold Corvette sitting under the overhang and ducked to check out the car's interior.

He walked through the lobby and across the dining terrace, seeing Wynn at the far end of the pool, a man lying at her feet. He double-timed across the pool deck and stopped, blinking, unable to believe his eyes: his wife's face and hands smeared in blood, the man at her feet unmoving, a dark streak spreading from the back of his head onto the concrete.

He scratched his brow, trying to summon sobriety, to gather his thoughts, to make sense of the scene. He gestured toward the man on the ground. "That your guy, there?"

Wynn nodded, still stunned.

Cabot pulled his phone from his pocket and offered it to her. "You should probably phone the *gendarmes*, don't you think?"

Chapter Seventeen

The priest stood in the shadow of the building, away from the wrought-iron railing, shivering. Estrella had put up a good fight. He had nearly got the upper hand before he went over the railing. It could as easily have been me down there, the priest thought. His left hand throbbed. He shook it out, and then picked the *bulto* off the balcony floor.

He stopped for a moment to admire the piece again, noticing that the outstretched arm had broken off in the fight. His heart sank a bit. The piece had survived intact for almost two hundred years, until tonight. He scanned the floor of the room, searching for the missing bit. When he couldn't find it, he nestled the San Lorenzo on a bed of cash in the gym bag and murmured a prayer of contrition. Even so, contrite as he was, he wasn't contrite enough to return the San Lorenzo to the cathedral in Tucson.

He squinted across the veranda. There was no back way out of the hotel except by the gate to the stables, and he wasn't sure he could find his way around to the front parking lot in the dark. He would have to go out the front door, passing guests and staff on the way. Still, if he had blood on his shirt, it was not of any great concern—his shirt was black; blood wouldn't show.

He sighed. The trip back to Arco Viejo would take more than an hour. He hated the drive up the twisting highway at this time of year, and especially if there was no moon to light the way. And the fucking coyotes would be out—nasty bastards looked like rocks in the road until they turned and snarled. Shit, that scared him—when the coyotes snarled.

He heard sirens approach and then go silent. He had to move. *Idiota*, the priest thought. His heart beat in his ears, until he realized the sound was someone knocking.

"*Señor?*" a woman's voice called. "*Señor?* This is turn-down service. I heard yelling, no? *Combate?* You are okay? I am coming in, okay?" The lock clicked, and a maid entered.

Deep in the shadows of the balcony, the priest doubled over behind a patio chair, curling his body around the precious gym bag, and flattened himself against the outside wall of the balcony.

"*Holá?*" the maid called out. She moved into the room. "*Holá?*" She saw the open balcony door and hurried to the balcony rail, and peered over, seeing Wynn haul Pablo Estrella's body from the pool. "*Que pas—Señor?*" she called down to the pool. "Are you okay?" When no answer came, she ran back to the phone in the room, snatched up the receiver, and punched zero. "*Emergencia,*" she cried to Eliu Colón at the front desk. "Get a doctor. I think a guest has fallen off the balcony!"

The priest heard the door close behind the maid. He stepped back inside and pulled the balcony door closed behind him. He ran a hand over his face, feeling for cuts, and then looked in the mirror over the dresser: the rims of his eyes were bloodshot from his angina, his pupils gold in the dusky light from the lamp near the door. He looked away and nodded. His eyes and an unbridled temper had given him the childhood nickname *Chupacabra*. The goat-sucker.

He took a tequila sampler from the minibar, his tongue yearning for something wet, and downed it straight from the bottle.

Without turning on the bathroom light, he splashed water on his face and squeezed a spot of Estrella's toothpaste onto his tongue. That would have to do until he got back to Arco Viejo.

Stepping out of the bathroom, he collided with Eliu Colón at the door.

"*Padré?*" Colón gasped. "Why are you here? What happened?" He trotted across the room, opened the balcony door, and leaned out over the rail.

Father Angel Hernandez followed Colón and came up behind him on the balcony. The tequila connected with the rush of adrenalin still coursing through his body. He lifted Colón up by the back of his shirt and the seat

CHAPTER SEVENTEEN

of his pants, aiming him over to the balcony railing. "I caught him stealing from the church. He angered God, and so I hit him."

Colón flailed in mid-air, feeling for the rail. "No one blames you, Father. But Sheriff Feliz does not need to find you here."

Hernandez knew that was true. He set Colón back down on the balcony. "You need to get the hell out of here, *Padré*. Now."

"What will you do?"

Colón smiled. "I have an idea." *Indeed, an inspired idea*, Colón thought—*one that would perhaps put Vista Cielo front-and-center in the news—and shine a light on the hotel. Why, it might be that a death would save the hotel's dying business.*

Chapter Eighteen

Feliz stood five paces from the corpse on the pool deck and glanced at his watch. He shifted a box of Cohiba cigars from one hand to the other. A smoker, a fundraiser he'd organized at Cheeks down in Santa Fe, was due to start in twenty minutes. If he didn't raise more than this five-hundred-dollar box of cigars had cost him, then something—something rash—would have to be done. And after all, these days, who really adhered to campaign finance laws?

Colón stepped to his elbow. "Two murders in as many days."

Feliz's shoulders sagged. "Worse than that, Iguanito. Three murders in four days. If I wanted to think so, I would blame Lisa and her *puta* attorney."

Colón licked his lips. "Ah, yes, the whore was killed too, wasn't she? But I think I have your answer, Ordierno. *Señor* Cabot checked in four days ago—*Señor* Phillip Cabot—of course, you have heard of him, yes?"

Out of the corner of his eye Feliz caught sight of Angel Hernandez skirting the dining terrace, walking toward the front of the building. He shook his head. "I do not pay much attention to the patrons of this hotel unless they cause trouble."

"No?" Colón smiled conspiratorially. "A wealthy developer from Texas, our *Señor* Cabot." He leaned in, lowering his voice. "I regret to tell you that Danilo sent *Señor* Cabot out to see"—he smiled coyly—"Alejandra Ramirez on the day he arrived. I believe he was her last…ah, client." He paused, waiting for Feliz to react. Nothing.

"And *Señor* Cabot's wife," Colón went on, "has been here many times with *Señor* Estrella. They would stay two, sometimes three or four days. This

CHAPTER EIGHTEEN

time? This time *Señor* Estrella is already here. He arrives the same day she..." Colón glanced over his shoulder as though he was about to share a great secret with Feliz. "Then there is this—I saw *Señora* Cabot in the gift shop only minutes before our man was killed. Coincidence, *que no?*" If Feliz agreed these were too many coincidences, Colon would kill two birds with one stone: give the sheriff a reasonable lead he could parlay into good campaign press and get the Cabot couple out of his hotel.

Only this morning, the bank had phoned—yet again—wanting to know when to expect the mortgage payment. The boiler needed servicing before winter came. And now this. The hotel had been his refuge from the time he was a teenager—his first job was at the valet desk, a job with a clean white uniform. A job at which he made some real money in tips, tips that bought his family's groceries after his bastard father died. He'd become the general manager. He was proud to work at Vista Cielo. The hotel was his home, but there were events and people who contrived to take all that from him.

Feliz sighed. The smoker would have to wait, dammit. He could always use more money for his campaign, but this crime wave had to be stopped or he would find himself cleaning out his desk to make room for DaShaye Williams.

Vista Cielo had begun to irritate him. Usually, nothing happened out here except the odd stolen laptop computer or a heart attack in a guest room, something that could be dealt with in a few minutes.

He handed the box of Cohibas to Colón. "Have the valet return these to Primo's on Sandoval and tell him to bring me the money." He pulled a notepad from his pocket. "I'll want to talk to witnesses, of course. But let us start with *Señora* Cabot."

Colón stood aside, gesturing with the cigar box toward the veranda. "Please, come with me."

Chapter Nineteen

Feliz paced behind the chair where Wynn sat, tapping a pen on his notepad. "You did not know Pablo Estrella?"

"Look, why am I a suspect? I tried to save that man from drowning. My husband and I are…"

"Yes, *Senór* Colón filled me in. You and your husband stay at the same hotel, but in different rooms, eh? To throw us off the scent? I'm having you moved up here, Mrs. Cabot, to your husband's room. It seems to be a new idea for you. Certainly, it makes it easier for me to keep an eye on you. You did not know Pablo Estrella?"

"No," she said.

Feliz stepped in front of her. "Look at my face, Mrs. Cabot. Do I look convinced? Do I have on my 'I believe you' smile?"

"I don't know what your 'I believe you' smile looks like." She pointedly looked away from him. "What I'm telling you is the truth. I didn't know *Señor* Estrella."

He scoffed. "I'm not a fool. Don't play me for one. You knew him."

"No."

"I say different. *Señor* Colón at the desk says different. Would you like us to run the security video of the last time you checked into Vista Cielo with Estrella?"

She lifted her chin. "All right, sure, I knew him."

Feliz stared at her while he chewed on an after-dinner toothpick. "Then why did you deny that when I first asked?"

"Because I realized how it would look if I admitted I knew him. And I

CHAPTER NINETEEN

didn't want my husband to find out that...that I knew him. And if you knew all this, why did you ask?"

"So, had you arranged to meet Estrella, then?" Feliz sniffed.

Wynn said nothing.

Feliz drummed his pen on the pad. "You've been at Vista Cielo with Estrella on several occasions, yes? Did you arrange to meet him there today?"

"No," she said. "I've already told you no. Frankly, I was surprised to find him here."

"And according to *Señor* Colón, your husband went off to be with one of our...local girls... night before last. Did you know that?" Feliz questioned her without looking up. "Don't you think it odd that shortly after your husband visited with her, she ended up dead? And you are found with a dead man that we can prove you knew. I think maybe you and your husband are on a killing spree. Is that right?"

"No, that's not true." She stepped to the sliding doors—her eyes going at once to the spot where she had knelt with Pablo.

"Mrs. Cabot, you are seen bending over the dead Pablo Estrella—a dead man who was your lover, *and you were the one who pulled him out of the pool*? How convenient." He stared at Wynn, studying her, and then turned away, aware that he was watching her mourn.

A deputy rolled a valet's cart into the room; Wynn's clothes hung on the rod, her luggage and toiletries among the multiple evidence bags piled beneath them.

Feliz sorted through the evidence bags and withdrew a *bulto* from one bag—a fine Saint Jude. His heart leaped. He knew this *bulto*. He inhaled, holding the breath while he thought. This piece had been Alejandra's—he had seen it many times. But something about the statue was different. It looked richer around the edges. What enhanced its colors? A matte burgundy in the creases and smears in the waves of flame in his crown. He turned the thing over, thinking, reaching for the answer. Part of it he already had. He had found Alejandra's Saint Jude, the patron saint of desperate causes, in the Cabot woman's room at Vista Cielo, a woman already suspected of murder. He could link her to Alejandra's killing as well as Estrella's with this saint stolen from Alejandra's bedside table.

Thank you, Jesus, he prayed. These were the times, and there had been so few of them in the last few years, when he felt like a real detective.

"Perhaps *Señor* Estrella leaned over his balcony, whispering to you about where to meet him later? Can he tell us what—oh, wait. *Señor* Estrella's dead. He can't tell us anything, can he?" He turned to DaShaye Williams standing at the door. "Keep an eye on Mrs. Cabot while I find her husband. I think I know where to look."

Chapter Twenty

Having given sleep up as a bad job, Seamus Caine flipped on the light, illuminating the largest of the twelve bedrooms in his Back Bay Boston mansion. He propped himself up just as his phone began to vibrate. He checked the readout and hit the button. "Wynn?"

"Seamus, I need your help." Her voice sounded far away in both distance and circumstance.

"I thought you were—on vacation." He spoke the word carefully. She had been irritated when he called to ask her to meet with the FBI agent. He wasn't going to ask how that had gone. He knew better.

"This is no vacation, believe me," Wynn said. "It's getting crowded with people I don't know and don't like, and the only one I knew and liked is dead." As quickly as she could, Wynn laid out what had happened.

Caine listened until she finished. "You're saying you *did* have a relationship with this man?" He got out of bed and paced while they talked.

"You know what Phillip's been like, Seamus. When I met Pablo Estrella he... He filled an empty space in my life."

"A moment... Are you talking about Pablo Estrella, the antiquities broker?"

"You know him? Well, of course, you would."

"I know of most everyone on that circuit. You're saying Estrella's dead?"

"Yes."

Caine sank onto the bed and leaned back against the pillows.

Damn Wynn for being so headstrong, he thought. *Like a basset hound, that woman. Maybe she got it from her mother or from fighting dyslexia all these years.*

He could tell she'd been offended when he suggested Phillip was guilty. She'd scoffed—her half-cough coming through quite clearly despite the crappy phone connection—and told him there was no way Phillip could have done it. Absolutely none.

Either she protested too much trying to convince herself of Phillip's innocence, or she really believed he wasn't the killer.

Oh, Wynn, you don't know him like I do, Caine thought, mentally running through his private dossier on Phillip Cabot. He'd followed Cabot's tomfoolery for years and kept an even closer eye on him since Wynn had married him—his personal records as well as all his business dealings, copies of his transcripts from grade school through that expensive eastern college from which his parents bought him a degree, the names of his women and their special… specialties. Those he'd bribed or gotten pregnant and paid off or left to fend for themselves. Yes, Caine could have told Wynn everything about Cabot down to the color of his pajamas and the way he'd voted in the last election.

He could have told her again, as he had on many occasions since she'd married him, Phillip Cabot was not a nice man. He would cause her grief and heartache. He knew Cabot better than his own wife did.

Caine took a sip of sparkling water with bitters to settle his stomach and sat back, thinking.

He could imagine her face dotted with those sweet freckles, the pleading in her beautiful green eyes that would, of course, match the frustration he heard in her voice.

He had said he would make a call—that he would try to help her. "But you're smart and resourceful, darling. That's why I hired you. Try to get some rest, and I'll talk to you again. Soon."

Chapter Twenty-One

Phillip Cabot slid onto what had become his usual stool in the hotel bar. Without asking, the bartender poured him two fingers of Gentleman Jack and set another Pacifico in front of the skinhead freak at the end of the bar. For a moment, the two drank in silence.

The skinhead belched quietly and said, "Somebody said she's your wife—the one who killed the guy out at the pool."

Cabot did not respond.

"I seen her here before, you know. With that guy. Guy she killed."

"She didn't kill him."

"She's pretty. Maybe pretty enough to get away with killing him, you know? Did you hear what I tol' you? She's been here with him before."

Cabot needed to shut this guy up, maybe shove the Pacifico bottle down the bastard's throat. "Yeah, I know." He looked toward the door of the bar and saw a small crowd around an attractive brunette who held a microphone and, behind her, a man with a television camera hoisted onto his shoulder. Next to them, a young man took photographs with his smartphone. The press had shown up.

Cabot had to get out of there. He pulled his money clip from his pants pocket, withdrew a twenty, and threw it on the bar. They'd be looking for him pretty quick if they had any nose at all for a story, and he didn't want to be seen ducking them.

He pulled another Jackson from the money clip and held it up in two fingers in front of the skinhead. "Is there a back door out of this place?"

The skinhead nodded in the direction of the restrooms. "Down that hall—the door at the end takes you directly to the guest rooms."

Cabot lifted the skinhead's Pacifico and put the twenty under it. "Buy yourself another. And you didn't see me in here, did you?"

"Mister, I never seen you before in my life."

Cabot decided he would pack and leave the hotel by the side door to the parking lot rather than through the lobby. Take a cab to the airport and call the front desk from there, tell them to leave the room on his credit card. Go to Wyoming or Oregon for a few days. Disappear down a rabbit hole. He hit the breaker bar and opened the door, which led not to the guest rooms but directly into the lobby. The skinhead's laughter echoed down the hallway.

A man approached, frowning. "Phillip Cabot?"

Cabot's heart raced. He recognized the guy as the man from the restaurant the previous evening and sensed that somehow he was in on this. Cabot had a hunch that "somehow" wasn't going to be good news. "Who's asking?"

Ordierno Feliz flashed his badge. "Cruz County Sheriff—please stop right there."

Cabot stepped back, feeling the full effect of his latest whack of Gentleman Jack. What a time to find out he'd told the wrong man to keep his fucking mouth shut at dinner last night.

Feliz took Cabot by the arm. "Come with me, please. We have what your wife would call 'an issue' with you."

Cabot sneered and pulled his arm away. "My wife takes issue with almost everything I do. You and I both know she took issue with how that dinner went last night, or didn't go."

"Mr. Cabot, you can make this easy or…" He motioned to an open elevator.

They rode in silence up to the second floor and walked down the U-shaped corridor, Feliz holding a tentative grasp on Cabot's elbow.

Cabot studied Feliz out of the corner of his eye: shorter than himself by almost a foot, the sheriff had patent-leather hair and large feet, giving him the general appearance of a hobbit. He supposed there might be a woman who thought Feliz handsome, though it was hard to understand what they would see in him other than the top of his head.

CHAPTER TWENTY-ONE

Halfway down the hall, Cabot paused, pulling out the card key for his room before he noticed a uniformed deputy standing just inside the open door. He caught a glimpse of Wynn standing on the room's balcony, staring at the pool terrace below. He grabbed at Feliz's jacket. "Wait—what is this?"

Feliz batted his hand away and steered Cabot into a room farther down the hall. Two cops stepped out, one from the bathroom, the second from within the bedroom, closing ranks to block his exit. Feliz pushed him toward a chair at the built-in desk.

Cabot's mind raced: he had to talk to Tripp. Trouble brewed here, and it had to do with the dead guy downstairs. This might be bigger trouble than whatever was going on in Houston, but it all added up to one helluva mess. And could they extradite to Texas in civil matters?

"As you know, *Señor* Cabot, two people have been killed here at Vista Cielo in the past two days, in addition to a woman I believe was an... ah... an acquaintance of yours."

Cabot smirked. "What? I don't know anything of the sort."

Feliz chuckled. "You know because we have three murders we can tie to you and your wife in the last four days."

The knot in Cabot's stomach relaxed. This didn't have anything to do with the mess in Houston. He chuckled. "My wife may think I'm a shit, but I'm no killer."

"No? Then, I guess she killed those people by herself. And I have evidence that puts one of you at the murder of Alejandra Ramirez. Do you recognize the name?"

Cabot shrugged. "Maybe. I met a woman named Alejandra a few nights back."

"The same, Mr. Cabot. Alejandra Ramirez."

Cabot gasped, feeling as though he'd been thumped between the shoulder blades by one of his front-end loaders. Damn, he thought. "That's...not possible."

"No? Given what we know, why not?"

"Be...well, because Wynn couldn't kill someone. She's wired differently from you and me—she has a problem. She doesn't do things right. She

83

couldn't murder somebody because she just wouldn't know how to go about it." He chuckled again. "It's the reason I sleep so well. Don't have to keep one eye open watching for the ol' meat-cleaver-in-the-head... you know?"

Feliz scribbled on his notepad. "Is her problem real, or is this something the two of you dreamed up?"

"Oh, no. It's quite real. A diagnosed thing. Check her medical records if you like. Dyseidetic dyslexia, it's called. She's pretty good until you ask her to plan a dinner party or organize a trip like this one or... well, almost anything. Then she can be the most scatterbrained critter you've ever met."

Feliz frowned. "Does she work, your wife?"

"She plays at working. Something to keep her entertained, not a real job. Works for an auction house. Appraises antiques, buys paintings, that sort of thing. Pays crap. I keep telling her she needs to quit and do what she should be doing."

"Which is?"

"You know, picking up my laundry, doing the charity circuit on my arm. You have to admit she's a good-looking woman. Around the house, she makes sure the maid and the gardener don't screw their Mexi... He gulped. "Uh, in general, she makes herself useful in wifely ways."

"We think, Mr. Cabot, that you had good reason to kill the last victim."

"Who was he, anyway?"

"Did I say the last one was a man?"

"No, but I mean, what sort of sorry son-of-a-bitch kills women? And why is it you think Wynn and I killed these folks?"

"As I said, we have evidence."

"Ah, you've got jack shit. If you had evidence, my wife wouldn't be standing in a room down the hall twirling her hair in her fingers. And you and I wouldn't be sitting here having this powwow. Wynn and I would be getting a free ride to wherever it is you keep your hoosegow."

Cabot leaned back in his chair and crossed his feet on the desk while he sized up Ordierno Feliz. How in the name of Sam Houston could the guy buy a sport coat with that kind of plaid in it? Wearing that thing was probably half the reason Feliz acted like a man who was trolling for a backhander—daring

CHAPTER TWENTY-ONE

somebody to insult that butt-ugly jacket. The other half of the prickly attitude might come from the lack-of-height thing.

He knew this kind of cop, knew they could be dangerous. Feliz had to leave with someone in handcuffs to maintain his reputation, but he would have to spring whoever he'd arrested once an alibi was confirmed. Cabot could concoct alibis at the drop of a sombrero—he'd done it all his life. He doubted Wynn could do the same. But spending a few hours in this guy's pokey would get Wynn off his radar—and he'd been pretty hard on Wynn that morning when he saw her leaving with the FBI agent. Maybe he owed her that much.

"Perhaps you would be interested to know what I found in Mrs. Cabot's room tonight?" Feliz waited.

"What would that be, pray tell? I can't begin to guess."

"The *bulto* from Alejandra Ramirez's bedside table. The murder weapon. The club that was used to kill her."

Shit, Cabot thought, frowning. What did that mean? That Wynn really had killed these people? How the hell else could that damned thing from Alejandra's get into Wynn's room? Okay,, maybe she killed Estrella—after all, she was bent over the body when the posse rode up. But what reason could she possibly have to kill some guy in a gift shop? Could she do that? Did she have the strength? And the Alejandra thing? Well, maybe she found out he'd gone out there and whacked her in a jealous rage. The thought made him smile, but it didn't sound like something Wynn would do at all. Cabot swung his feet off the desk. "All circumstantial. Doesn't prove a thing."

Feliz shook his head. He smiled as though he had scored in this contest of wits. "I disagree, Mr. Cabot. Indeed, I think it looks very bad for your wife. I would say we will be taking her into custody shortly, probably booking her for all three murders."

"You're just itching to arrest someone, aren't you, Feliz? Okay, then, arrest me. You know what'd happen to my wife in your shit-hole of a jail, and so do I. It'd undo her, her head wired like it is."

Feliz tapped his pencil on the pad. "You have experience in our jails, *señor*?"

Leaning back in the chair again, Cabot laced his fingers behind his head.

"I spent a couple of days in the Española jail when I was sixteen, drunk as a poet on bad tequila. But I learned more than one lesson from that—among other things, I saw what could happen to a woman in a New Mexico jail."

He waited, listening to the sounds of evening float up from outside: voices from the terrace, the trumpet and guitars of the mariachi band in the restaurant. Almost eleven at night and still with the everlasting "Ayyy, yi, yi yi."

"Perhaps you want to call a lawyer?"

Cabot's shoulders slumped. What could you expect from an ass but a kick in the balls? He reached for the wad of money in his jacket pocket. "Women are on this earth for three reasons, Feliz." While he talked, he pulled out the top desk drawer, withdrew the Gideon Bible, and opened it as if to read scripture. Instead, he slipped five one-hundred-dollar bills from the money clip between its pages and closed the cover. "They walk this earth to sap our energy, suck the life out of our wallets, and laugh at us when we're naked."

He slid the bible across the desk toward Feliz. "Don't take Mrs. Cabot to your shit-hole jail. Keep her here, and I guarantee she won't walk. If she does, there's plenty more where that came from. Cuff her to the bed or the bathroom plumbing, if you like. But please… let her stay here."

Feliz took the bible, quickly tucked the hundred-dollar notes into his pants pocket, and threw it on the bed. He smiled to himself—Phillip Cabot had just assured his reelection. No investigation, no searches necessary; they had a suspect who came forward willingly and turned himself in. "Officers," he said at last. "Arrest this man." He pulled Cabot to his feet. "You have *cojonés grandés* if you're taking the blame for this to save your wife."

Cabot was a strange man, Feliz thought. But if he was out of the picture, his wife would have no choice. Women who were alone were easier to break. And Mrs. Cabot would be no problem, he thought. She was a godless woman who treated men as badly as his ex-wife had. Another woman of independent mind.

Feliz knew a few like that, most of them women he worked with. He didn't like them. He was, after all, a creature of great God-given violence.

CHAPTER TWENTY-ONE

Women could sense that. Some women liked violent men, men of spirit and machismo. Those like Mrs. Cabot and Lisa and the women he worked with, they apparently did not. Those women were the most enjoyable to break.

Cabot shook his head and looked away as the cops put him in handcuffs. "Wynn and I have a muddy horsepond of a marriage, Feliz. The whole deal is nothing but a goddamned muddy horsepond."

For a moment, Feliz almost sympathized with Cabot—he'd known a goddamned muddy horsepond of a marriage himself when he and Lisa Guzman eloped in the summer before she started law school. For a month or so, they'd had the kind of marriage he had thought they might, and then Lisa began to have other ideas of who the boss was in their relationship. After she started law school, things got worse—Lisa began telling him when he could go out and with whom, how much money he could spend on his clothes and what kind he should buy, and then she began nagging at him to take a second job as a security guard, and a third, working night shift in a burger joint, to pay her tuition, to keep her in Armani suits, to pay for her nail appointments and a princess-cut diamond ring. And after she graduated law school, she became almost unrecognizable as the girl he had courted on the *banco* in the plaza of Arco Viejo the summer they were both seventeen.

Chapter Twenty-Two

FBI agent André Bishop double-timed his green Ford out to Vista Cielo, glancing at his beat-up Timex every three or four minutes. He'd fallen asleep around six that evening while he watched *Singin' in the Rain*. He thought he would nap for an hour and still have plenty of time to prepare before his meeting with Pablo Estrella at nine. Now it neared eleven o'clock, and he hoped he hadn't blown it. Estrella had said he had information about the original Zuni San Gabriel, but he didn't want to talk over the phone—he'd insisted that they meet in his room at the hotel.

He rounded the corner off Highway 86 and pulled up under the *porté-cochère* at Vista Cielo, parking behind a Cruz County patrol car that sat at the entrance. He cut the engine, collected his notebooks, and looked up, surprised to see Wynn Cabot's husband being hustled out the front door by a man with slicked-down hair and a swashbuckler of a moustache—a real Errol Flynn kind of guy. Except for his size.

Bishop left his car where it sat and approached the patrol car. "FBI, sir," he said and opened his ID case.

Feliz scoffed. "This is a local case, Agent"—Feliz peered at the ID—"oh, *Special* Agent Bishop of the Art Crimes Unit. Nothing to concern you here."

"I think there is. This man's wife is part of an investigation I'm conducting."

"Yes? You are…ah…familiar with Mrs. Cabot? As so many men seem to be?"

"Shut the fuck up!" Cabot reared and swung his handcuffed hands at Feliz's head, managing only to flick a strand of Feliz's shiny hair out of place.

Bishop grabbed Cabot by his elbows, pivoted him away from Feliz, sat him

CHAPTER TWENTY-TWO

down in the patrol car, gave him a shove, and closed the patrol car door. He turned again to the sheriff. "Now then. Who are you?"

Feliz patted his hair back into place and pulled out his own badge folder. "Sheriff Ordierno Feliz, Cruz County. Mr. Cabot is coming with me."

"Well, for the moment, maybe. After that, we'll see, won't we?"

"I can tell you there is nothing for you to investigate." Feliz chuckled. "No"—he waggled fingers in air quotes—"'art crime' here."

"You never know."

"What brings you to Vista Cielo so late, *Special* Agent Bishop?"

"A meeting—oddly, a meeting about an art crime. An appointment for which I'm very late."

Feliz took in a breath. Instinct told him Bishop's very presence here in New Mexico had something to do with the recent rash of murders. He ventured a guess. "Ah. With Pablo Estrella?"

"Yeah. With Pablo Estrella."

"I'm sorry to say, *Special* Agent Bishop, you will not need to worry about being late for your appointment. Estrella was killed this evening. By Mr. Cabot. Or Mrs. Cabot—we are not sure which. Mr. Cabot has confessed, and so that is that. Case open and shut. Mrs. Cabot, however, is not yet allowed to leave the hotel, until we process her husband's confession."

Bishop drew in a breath and let it out slowly, thinking, frowning. Estrella was dead, and the Cabotes were suspects. Well then, Mrs. Cabot needed his help as much as he needed hers. He pulled himself up tall in front of Feliz.

Feliz leaned in and clenched his teeth. "She will not leave."

"Mosquito," Bishop said between his teeth. "She might, if we need to go somewhere."

"She does, and I will deal with you. If Mrs. Cabot leaves, she'll be with me."

Chapter Twenty-Three

From a window in the second-floor stairwell, Wynn watched the men below. The body language between Bishop and Feliz was palpable two floors up—especially the sheriff's. *Well,* she thought, as Feliz drove away with Cabot in tow, *that's one way to ditch a husband for a while—pack him off to the chill factory.* Still, she knew her husband, and she doubted he'd be gone for long.

He'd be in the slammer for a few hours, and then they'd turn him loose because, of course, he would have some sort of an alibi for all this. Her husband wasn't as hammer-headed as some people thought. She had no doubt he'd handicapped his odds before he let Detective Dwarf put him in wristlocks. And when he came back, he'd be mad as a cat in a bomber jacket, wanting answers she didn't yet have.

When Bishop asked for the number of Wynn Cabot's room, Eliu Colón raised an eyebrow and made a point of checking the clock on the wall behind him. Colón had seen Bishop before—in the lobby a couple of days ago, talking with Mrs. Cabot—and he'd watched as Bishop and Feliz talked outside. He could tell the conversation hadn't gone well for the sheriff.

Bishop flashed his FBI ID and asked again. Colón fidgeted at his keyboard, stalling, thinking. "I can phone the guard on her room and let him know you are here. But really, it's after eleven."

"Of course. Tell him the FBI won't let her go anywhere—for the moment. Is the restaurant open?"

"The restaurant, no, but you could talk in the bar." Yes, Colón thought, the

CHAPTER TWENTY-THREE

bar. The bar. Always the bar.

When Wynn Cabot walked into the bar, Bishop gasped, just as he had when he first saw her. She had such an air, this one. Moved like silk. She sat beside him with tears glittering in her lashes.

"Pablo said when he phoned last night that he was meeting someone at nine tonight." She closed her eyes. "A man, he said. 'I have a man coming to see me later, but I should be done by ten.' So that was you. How did you know him?"

"I got his number from the curator at the Folk Art Museum yesterday. She'd just taken delivery of the Zuni San Gabriel when I showed up asking questions. She thought Estrella and I should talk."

"Of course. Yes, he told me he'd sold them the piece."

"But then how did you end up standing there when…"

"I'd gone out to the pool to think. About Phillip—after he was so rude to you yesterday morning—"

"He was rude to *you,* and then he got feisty with me."

She nodded. "So I'd wanted some time—it's the reason I came here." She frowned and pulled a tissue from her handbag. "Your nose is bleeding."

"Thanks. It's the air, I think. Dry." Bishop took the tissue and tipped his head back. "Anyway, go on."

"So I was out at the pool, trying to think. And then I heard a noise on a balcony above me, and I looked up just as Pablo fell. Look, isn't there something the FBI can do about this? Can't you—"

"Murder isn't usually a federal case, Mrs. Cabot."

"Wynn. Please call me Wynn."

Bishop gave a quick frown. "So… You knew Pablo?"

Wynn pressed her lips together. "Yes. Had known him. We did business together a couple of times."

Bishop nodded. He didn't want to speculate on the sort of business Wynn Cabot was speaking of. "So Estrella's dead, and Feliz thinks you did it?"

She nodded. "I guess. Even though he's arrested Phillip, there are still guards at my door."

"Look," Bishop dabbed again at his nose. "Feliz thinks maybe you shouldn't leave the hotel. I don't think so either, but for a different reason. If you leave, you might be corralled by whoever killed Estrella. After all, whoever did this might think you're a witness. Witnesses are dangerous to a murderer."

Wynn returned to her room, glancing at the bedside clock: a few minutes before midnight. Maybe the police would hold Phillip until morning. She could get a few hours' sleep.

She stepped out onto the balcony and leaned on the wrought-iron rail, inhaling air perfumed by star jasmine that clung to the exterior walls and the scent of coconut suntan lotion that lingered from the pool area directly below. She stared blankly, remembering, barely glancing at the familiar view of the mountains silhouetted against the moonlit sky and the wide black desert spread at their feet. Weariness finally settled in, and she secured the sliding glass doors, cranked the air conditioning down to Frigid Bitch, and tried to sleep. But every time she closed her eyes, she saw Pablo lying on the pool deck, his mouth open, his eyes staring at the sky.

I loved you, you deceived me, I loved you, you deceived me, the air conditioner gargled.

She lay watching shadow patterns of the pool lights swim on the ceiling. She couldn't think straight; the dyslexia that was so often a curse also offered an unexpected gift in some situations, and this was one: it enabled her to see a puzzle from all angles, studying it in three dimensions.

But the exercise raised more questions than it answered. First, was Pablo killed, or was it an accident? Or, even more unthinkable, suicide?

For one thing, Pablo's body was limp when she pulled him out of the pool. Drunk perhaps? Not likely. In the two years she'd known him, she'd never seen him touch alcohol.

She replayed the scene again in her mind. Her heart twisted each time she saw him lying by the pool, but she had to think it through. Was it, then, an accident? There had been…something else. What?

She sat up, cross-legged on the bed, burying her face in her hands, pushing herself to remember. She'd heard noises…of a scuffle when she went to the

CHAPTER TWENTY-THREE

pool, sounds of balcony furniture striking the rail, a groan, a slap, a gasp, someone swearing. So he might have been in a fight.

Then there was his head wound…. "No," she cried out and leaped off the bed, shaken. She finally had the answer she sought but had struggled not to see. He had received the blow to his head before he fell.

Chapter Twenty-Four

Phillip Cabot sat in a far corner of the holding cell, a gang-banger his only company. Feliz strutted in front of the cell, a white silk sport coat draped over his shoulders in a mannered way that lowered him even further in Cabot's estimation. *Relax*, he thought. *This little bastard's more than a few cattle shy of a roundup.*

"You see, Mr. Cabot,"—Feliz flashed his Cartier watch for Cabot's benefit—"the situation is even bigger than we imagined. We have proof that your wife had been seeing *Señor* Estrella for…well, for quite some time."

He paused, and then leaned in to deliver the news: "As a matter of fact, your wife and *Señor* Estrella came to Vista Cielo on several occasions for their…ah, enjoyment." He braced, waiting for Cabot to explode.

Cabot didn't flinch. What Feliz thought was news, Cabot had already surmised from seeing Wynn with the guy at the stables. The skinhead at the bar had confirmed it. He chuckled. "Take your faggy ass out of here, Feliz. I resent your thinking I'd buy that."

Feliz cocked an eyebrow, surprised by Cabot's self-control. "Suit yourself, Mr. Cabot. I can have Eliu Colón, the hotel manager, bring the registration logs down to show you, if you like. That would give you dates for their visits, so you could check for yourself to see if she was out of town. Oh, and the photographer at the restaurant—the lovely woman who takes photos of people on their idyllic vacations—you know the one? She has shots of your wife and Estrella over candlelight dinners on the terrace."

"Yeah, yeah, yeah. Get out of here and, on your way, tell the bailiff I could use a shave and a shot of bourbon."

CHAPTER TWENTY-FOUR

"You are a long way from a shave and a shot, *Señor* Cabot."

Feliz smiled to himself. Maybe he would also convict this idiot gringo for the murder of Alejandra. Why, perhaps right here in his jail was the son of a bitch who had fed his friend bourbon, tied her hands to the bedposts before he took her, and then he killed her.

"I told you, Feliz, I didn't kill him. Neither did my wife. And take off that jacket—with your floppy feet and that silly-ass jacket, you look like Niko Liko."

Feliz lunged for Cabot through the bars of his cell, the silk jacket falling to the floor. "You *puta* piece of shit—I don't pay for my women. They *give* me what I want."

Cabot ducked his grab and danced away, grinning and shadowboxing through the bars of the cell. "Niko Liko, Feliz. That's who you are—a cop in clown clothes."

"*Chingate*—you have no idea who I am, Cabot," Feliz shouted, bending to pick up his jacket. "But keep it up, and you'll find out." He shook out the jacket and approached, reaching through the bars but managing to grab only the gangbanger, twisting the top of his pants and pulling him to the front of the cell.

"Ow," the kid protested, "stop that."

Feliz snarled in the kid's face. "You are in my house, Alberto. You do not tell me what to stop. So I ask you again, do you want to tell me why you had all those syringes, or do you want to skip your dinner?"

"I told you—I have diabetes. I need my insulin—*please*, Sheriff."

"You are not diabetic, Alberto. I have watched you for years—you're not using those syringes on yourself, and we both know it. Tell me or your friend over in the corner there, Mr. Cabot, he gets your dinner."

"I need food, Sheriff—something to keep my blood sugar going—"

"You get food when you tell me why you had those syringes in a bag. No one walks around my county with a bag full of syringes, *comprende*?" Feliz threw the kid away from the bars. "You think about it for a few minutes, and I'll be back to see if your diabetes has gone away."

***

Tossing back the covers, Wynn swung her feet to the floor, went to the sliding glass doors, and out onto the balcony. Daylight had begun to color the sky. Below, at the end of the pool deck where she'd pulled Pablo from the water, she saw nothing. No chalk marks outlining where a body had been, no bloodstain on the concrete pool deck to indicate that anything had occurred there the night before. The whole thing had been erased, as though Pablo's death was nothing more than a mistake in a crossword puzzle.

It seemed Sheriff Feliz had already made up his mind about who had killed Pablo, and what if he was right? What if Phillip really was the killer? Wynn frowned. He had, after all, been at her side shortly after she'd pulled Pablo from the pool.

Why would he go to the trouble? Certainly not out of jealousy. Could she level with Feliz about the state of her marriage? And, if she did—if she used the excuse of estrangement to get Phillip off the hook—would Feliz believe her, especially at this point?

She couldn't leave solving this mess to Feliz and Bishop. If something didn't happen, and soon, she and Phillip might be lost in the prison system for weeks—or longer—and, if one of them was convicted, longer still. She had to do something.

She cracked open the door to her room and peered out. The guard, stationed in an armchair five feet away, dozed. Quickly she donned the terry cloth bathrobe, wrapped her hair in a towel, grabbed her room key, slipped into the hall, and headed toward the opposite wing of the hotel. A housekeeping cart stood in front of Estrella's room, the door propped open with a rolled towel. Wynn slowed as she walked by, studying the layout: a mirror image of her own room.

A maid stripped the sheets off Estrella's bed and moved to the bathroom, where she grabbed towels off a rack. She sang distractedly while she worked.

Wynn pulled her room key from her pocket, pretending to unlock the room next door. She waved and called, *"Holá,"* as the maid pulled the rolled towel from the door jamb and wrestled the load of linens down the hall

CHAPTER TWENTY-FOUR

to the laundry. Wynn caught the door before it closed and slipped into Estrella's room, glancing first into the bathroom. She wrinkled her nose. The room reeked as though the maid had gone over every inch of it with bleach. Toiletries lay in a neat row on the glass shelf above the sink, but no dop kit sat nearby.

She moved on to the main room. In a sitting area near the balcony, blood had seeped into the grout between the saltillo tiles. Three receipts lay on the bedside table, one from the gift shop downstairs for a *santo*, the second from the Five and Dime General Store on the plaza where Pablo had bought a razor, toothpaste, and a toothbrush. The third—she heard a sound, as though someone approached.

She went to the door and checked both directions. Empty and quiet, except for the hum of a washing machine in the laundry room. She turned again and stared into the room. Pablo had favorite hiding places in rooms like this, she knew: the undersides of drawers or between a mattress and its box spring, but a quick search of the dresser drawers showed nothing, either in them or under them.

She moved to the bed, bracing her feet to lift the heavy mattress. Once again, nothing. She lowered the mattress and looked around, then reached down between the bed and the nightstand to retrieve a piece of wood the shape, size, and color of a Maduro cigar. The wooden piece turned out to be carved like an arm, the fingers of its hand outstretched.

She slid aside the closet door. Nothing inside except the usual: an iron and ironing board on the right-hand wall, two terry robes hanging at the opposite end, a safe on the floor, pillows on the shelf, and...wait. What was that between the pillows?

She jumped up, catching the edge of the shelf with her right hand, stretching her left arm toward the object, still barely able to skim the surface with her fingertips. She tugged at the lower pillow, trying to pull the piece closer. Dear God, she thought, don't let me bring this whole thing down on my head. Fingers trembling, she secured a grip on the piece, yanked it from the shelf, and gasped. A *bulto*, a Saint Joseph. And obviously not missing an arm.

She studied it closely—yes, this was the second of the two she had shown the gift shop manager on the afternoon he was killed.

She tucked the carving inside her robe, stuffed the receipts and the wood arm in a bathrobe pocket, and ducked out, rounding the corner to her own room just as the maid emerged from the laundry with fresh linens.

The guard startled awake as Wynn came down the hall. "Good morning," she said. "Went for a swim—didn't see any point in wakening you." She slid her room key in the slot and smiled at the deputy. "Did you sleep well?"

Wynn squinted at the third receipt, trying to make the letters hold still, to arrange themselves into words she knew. Damn it, she thought, this is a bad time for the dyslexia to kick in. Did that read Chicken Itza or Kitchen Itza? Whichever it was, the receipt, from a restaurant in Tucson, Arizona, was dated three weeks ago and, judging from the amount of the tab, he'd eaten alone. She didn't know the place.

She studied the disembodied wooden arm. Obviously broken off a *bulto*. The carved detail on the fingers of the hand was superb, reminding her of the work of Ignacio Garza.

She rubbed the Saint Joseph, trying to pick up any impression Pablo might have left on the piece. She could sometimes sense the feelings others infused in their possessions, the things she brokered for the auction house. But she felt nothing other than the sensation that had settled last night between her shoulder blades, as though she was cold from her core out.

She stood, rolled the *santo* into a dry cleaning bag and nestled it behind a spare blanket in a drawer, tucked the wood arm and the gift shop receipt in her handbag, and headed downstairs.

At a table in the hotel restaurant, Ordierno Feliz tried to steady his hand as he forked a pile of *huevos motuleños* into his mouth. He still seethed over the thought that Phillip Cabot had been the last person to see Alejandra Ramirez alive.

He tapped the fork against his lips, trying to bring a thought forward; something in the back of his mind that had nagged at him since last night, something else that had to do with the dead men. Feliz had seen the man

CHAPTER TWENTY-FOUR

from the gift shop somewhere else, but could not place where.

Another mouthful of eggs and tortilla washed down with *jugo* and *café* did nothing to jog his memory. He saw photos of hundreds of criminals every year; maybe the gift shop manager just looked familiar. Estrella he knew, of course. Had known. Briefly.

Still, there was something about the dead man in the gift shop—his face kept popping up whenever Feliz was not concentrating on other details—something about that guy struck a chord.

An image snapped to the front of his mind as though fired from a slingshot: that guy had been the subject of a bulletin sent out—what? Six months ago?—by the FBI. Usually, the Feds confined themselves to mobsters and corrupt government officials, interstate drug trafficking, and armored-car thefts. The Ten Most Wanted. They issued notices to police departments about stolen goods. Terrorists. The usual crap. Made the Fibbies feel like they'd done something toward the war on crime, he thought. What a bunch of white-collar pussies. Why, it had taken them sixteen years to find Whitey Bulger.

But one of the notices carried the photo of a man who hadn't made the big ten. The photo clearly showed a horizontal scar running from the man's right nostril across his cheek to the bottom of his right earlobe. Along with the photo had been the usual statistics—a number of burglaries, including religious treasures he'd stolen from churches—but the bothersome bit was that in doing so, he had killed a couple of parish priests who'd tried to fight back.

Even more than that, he'd known the guy—worked with him in the days he and Estrella muled for the cartel. Colón would never hire such a man to manage his gift shop—and the cartel knew it.

A guy like that couldn't be trusted with tourists, so he would have had to come from somewhere else, an outsider standing in for the manager, a dodge.

Feliz flipped the peas out of his eggs while he thought.

Colón had been one step ahead of him and put in a stooge. He'd seen the gift shop's manager had a target on his back, and put someone else—someone close and expendable—in his place.

El Eché had killed the wrong man.

And if Estrella had been using the gift shop as a clearing house for the *bultos* and *retablos* he'd swindled from the churches but couldn't sell to museums or collectors, then there was this question: how had he come up with the money for his purchases? And, more interesting, where would he stash his profits?

Feliz finished his coffee and stood. He needed more information, and he knew where to get it.

Chapter Twenty-Five

Two minutes later, he stood in the hotel's second-floor hallway. "Mrs. Cabot," he called, as he knocked sharply on her door. No answer. He knocked and called again. "Mrs. Cabot, Cruz County Sheriff Ordierno Feliz. Open up, please."

The maid appeared in a doorway down the hall. "Sir?"

"Mrs. Cabot, open this door."

Shrugging, the maid came forward. "I can open it, but she is not there."

"She left? How long ago?"

The maid thought. "Fifteen, maybe twenty minutes ago."

"She did not leave the hotel?"

She shrugged again. "How would I know? I did not see."

Feliz turned for the elevator, then decided the stairs would be faster.

There she was. Feliz strode into the dining room and stopped behind Wynn Cabot. "Mrs. Cabot," he said and took her by the elbow. "Let's get a coffee. I have some questions about your line of work."

Wynn hesitated. "Agent Bishop is in charge of the investigation into the counterfeit *bultos*, Sheriff. If you have questions, please see him. I believe he is in Santa Fe, at the Budget Inn Express on Cerrillos Road."

"This has nothing to do with counterfeit *bultos*, Mrs. Cabot. I want to talk about what you might know about the real thing. You seem very interested in our carvings."

He held a chair for her that would seat her facing Pablo's balcony. Wynn feigned not to notice the courtesy and pulled out a chair that faced the gate to the stables instead.

For a woman whose husband thinks she has a scattered brain, Feliz thought, she is smarter than Phillip Cabot knows. "Tell me," he said. "The *bultos*. Are they a hobby?"

"They're more than that to me. We deal with them at the auction house I work for."

He nodded. "You sell them for decoration?"

"Not usually. I sell to collectors. Those who appreciate what the *santos* represent—well, not only the saint, but what the saint stands for, and the faith. Most of my clients for *santos* are Catholic."

Feliz ordered two coffees.

"What my buyers appreciate," Wynn went on, "is a well-crafted carving that shows the temperament of the saint as well as the love that the carver himself—or herself, sometimes—puts into the statue. For my clients, it's fun to imagine this statue being carried at the head of a procession...."

"A *cortejo*."

"Yes. It's moving to think of devout people dressing this icon in clothes of beautiful fabrics and parading it through the streets. My buyers visualize the rituals in their imaginations. They sense the smells of the flowers and incense that surround the procession. And the music of people singing and playing the drum, and the happy pop of fireworks. That's what my customers buy when they buy a *santo*. They don't buy decorations."

The waiter set a coffee pot and two cups on the table.

"But the *santo* trade in this area is..." Feliz waggled his hands. "How do you say it? Good and bad together."

She nodded. "A mixed bag."

"Exactly. Most of the *santos* sold here are made for tourists."

Wynn cocked an eyebrow. "And some of them are legitimate—quite valuable."

Feliz reached across the table and laid a hand on hers. "But only an expert could tell if a statue is a treasure or not."

She looked down at his hand, slipped hers from underneath it, and picked up her coffee cup. "That's not a problem."

CHAPTER TWENTY-FIVE

"No?"

"No," she said. "Because I am an expert."

Feliz leaned back in his chair. "Then I am telling you things you already know. Perhaps I can call upon you with future cases."

Smiling at him over the rim of the cup, she said, "Then you'll have to come to Houston. After the last few days, I hope not to be spending much more time here."

"It would be my pleasure to come to Houston," he said, surprised that he meant it. Yes, it *would* be a pleasure, he thought. For a moment, he yearned only to caress her smooth, pale skin. He shivered slightly, knowing Pablo Estrella had done that very thing, and he began again. "This Pablo Estrella, then? Was he one of your…clients?"

"As I said, I worked with him on a couple of things."

"Ah, yes. What…*things*?"

She sighed. "He wanted me to appraise some *santos* he'd bought for a museum."

"And you did this?"

She nodded.

"When did you start—"

"Pablo called me a bit over a year ago, asking about a Mary, *Nuestra Señora de la Soledad*. He emailed me a picture."

Feliz took a deep breath. This was the woman for whom Estrella tried to leave the cartel? Could it be she didn't know his past? "I mean," Feliz said, "when did you establish… more personal relations?"

"Mmm." She shut her eyes for a moment, remembering. "He came to an auction at Caine—where I work—in Houston, in February of last year. He brought several photos of an entire Holy Family carving. I needed time to study the pictures, so we met on several occasions."

"A *santo* like that, what would it be worth?"

"Wrong question."

"How do you mean, wrong question?"

"A work of art, whether it's carved wood or carved marble, or paint on canvas or a pencil drawing, isn't worth very much in itself. I mean, what is a *bulto*? Cheap materials, basically: a chunk of wood, some inexpensive paint. Maybe some gold leaf for inspiration and razzle-dazzle. But its worth comes when there is someone who wants it. So the proper question is, what is its value to a buyer? To a decorator, it's a few hundred dollars. To a collector, the value for a good one increases to thousands, maybe tens of thousands, sometimes hundreds of thousands. But, of course, to the faithful who parade it in the *cortejo* or *procesión*, it's priceless."

Feliz nodded and gave a cynical chuckle. "How well I learned that lesson. I bought a picture once—a picture of a very fat dancer. I liked the picture well enough, but the man who owned the gallery—Hampton Gallery, do you know it?—he said it was worth much more than its price, and that it was from a collector in Florida who wanted to sell it quickly." He sighed. "Oh, that guy, what a snow job—isn't that the term?—he gave me. Took me to dinner at a steakhouse downtown that night, 'only the best,' he said. I should have known right then."

Wynn smiled sympathetically. "Did he say the piece was by Botero?"

"Exactly. How did you know?"

"Botero is one of the most forged painters in the world. Or was. The stories of Botero forgeries are legend. Collectors became so suspicious of Boteros that the value of his work has dropped dramatically. I'm sorry about your piece."

Feliz shrugged. "It covers a hole in one wall in my living room. And I still like it. But I found out it isn't worth even what I paid for it. Not even the signature is in the right place."

They walked down the second-floor hallway toward her room. Feliz tried to figure out what he wanted to say, finally settling on, "Frankly, Mrs. Cabot, *Señor* Estrella had come to my notice long before you or your husband killed him."

Wynn drew in a breath but waited, though she had already guessed what was going on. Feliz was asking different questions—odd questions—about Pablo because he wanted something else. But if he had Phillip in custody for killing Pablo, why was he back at all? And why did he walk like a duck?

CHAPTER TWENTY-FIVE

Feliz continued, "Estrella was not in a legitimate business, you know."

She considered her words carefully. "He purchased those statues from parish priests. He did not steal them."

"Some of them he bought. Others he stole, when he had the opportunity," Feliz said. "You knew what he was doing, *que no?*"

"I found out three, four months ago." She blinked back tears. "When he let it slip, I—I couldn't reconcile the thought of being with another man who was as deceitful as my husband. And then I wondered, was I being just as deceptive in doing business with him? That's when I broke off our relationship."

He touched her arm again, not as he did in his official capacity, but gently took her arm, stroking it with his thumb, hoping he touched her heart as well. His sudden surge of feeling for her had nothing to do with this interrogation.

Surprised at the way he touched her, she started, pulling her arm away. "I'm worried about Phillip."

Feliz stepped back, surprised that she didn't seem interested in his affection. "And he is worried about you."

"Is he okay?"

"Cruz County has a large, modern jail. I assure you, Mr. Cabot is not suffering."

"Believe me, if he can't wander around telling other people how to live their lives, he's suffering. Have you charged him yet?"

"We think Mr. Cabot went to visit *Señor* Estrella, and they fought—perhaps about you. But the ME has discovered *Señor* Estrella died of a blow to the head—the unfortunate outcome of a crime of passion. If that's right, your *esposo* could be released very quickly."

He stopped for a moment and watched her, expecting her to react. Nothing—no gasp, no concern for her own safety or freedom. Perhaps she really hadn't killed Estrella. He continued walking while he said, "Yes, we would release your husband and arrest you."

They stopped at the door to her room. Feliz studied her. She was a curious creature—this woman with easy morals. She had slept with at least one other man besides her husband, but she seemed to miss her thickheaded jerk.

Still, she was young, she must have needs. It was not unreasonable to hope. Gently, he reached up and took her hand, then stretched, trying to stand tall enough to kiss her.

She pulled her hand away, feeling in her bag for her room key. My god, she thought. Did Feliz just try what I think he tried?

Feliz's face flushed. He had never had a woman refuse him before. "All saint and no sinner, Mrs. Cabot?"

"What? What does that mean?"

"You know what I mean. You were seen going into the gift shop the afternoon the manager of the shop was killed."

Wynn pushed a lock of auburn hair out of her face. "Yes, I went in to see the *santos*."

"And what did you purchase?"

"A *bulto*."

"Just so," Feliz said. "Apparently you were the last person to see the man alive."

"He is the man who died the night before Pablo was killed?"

"You pretend you don't know?"

"I didn't know."

"Another man is dead—killed the same way as your lover."

"We've covered that ground already," Wynn said. "I didn't hit Pablo, and I didn't hit… whoever he is. Was."

"I know you—" No, he thought. Don't use Alejandra yet. Save that one. "Yes. As you say."

"Can I see Phillip?"

"No. I told you—you may not leave the hotel."

"I don't believe that's quite the way Agent Bishop sees it."

Feliz turned to leave and glanced over his shoulder. "Pah," he scoffed, throwing back his head and righting the lapels of his suit jacket as he strode down the hallway.

Chapter Twenty-Six

Ordierno Feliz stood in his fury once again—anger radiating out to the tips of his fingers as he drove to the Budget Inn Express on Cerrillos Road in Santa Fe. He identified himself to the front desk clerk and learned that Bishop had the room next to the ice machine. Perfect, Feliz thought—far enough from the hotel office and maybe noisy enough to cover whatever might transpire when he got past Bishop's front door.

He tapped lightly on the door and listened, hearing the low murmur of a television set from within. Music and stilted dialogue. An old movie, from the sound of it. "Agent Bishop," he called. "Cruz County Sheriff Feliz here. Open the door, please."

Feliz looked around, hoping the hotel maids were working on the upper floor. He didn't want witnesses. He felt his wrath subside in the cool morning air and worked to summon it again, but could not risk attracting attention by pounding on the door. He went back to the office, picked up the lone house phone, and asked to be connected to Bishop's room. The phone rang unanswered.

Now he was really pissed. He needed to get into that room—if Bishop wasn't there, he'd toss the place and find out what gave with that guy. He strode across the small lobby to the front desk and flashed his badge. "Need to get into André Bishop's room."

The young East Indian man barely looked up from the book he was reading—a book on tort law. "Cruz County? You got a search warrant? Because I don't think you have jurisdiction over here."

"I can have a warrant in five minutes, and get you fired in ten."

"I don't think so, sir. I own the place."

"You don't know who I am, do you?"

"Sure I do. I've seen the signs. You're running for Sheriff out in Cruz County. One of the guys running, anyway. I don't think you're going to win, but that may be just me not liking your attitude."

Feliz's face purpled. He had to get out of the hotel office before he started shooting the place up. Just then, he spotted the green government-issue Ford sedan pulling into a parking place adjacent to the ice machine. He threw open the door of the hotel office. "Bishop!" He unsnapped the strap on his holster and withdrew his Beretta service pistol. This candy-assed agent would pay for the humiliation he had just been handed by some dot-headed frat boy who owned a cheap-ass motel and thought he could sass a sheriff. Feliz would show these assholes how law enforcement really did business.

Bishop got out of his car, glanced in Feliz's direction, and held his hands out and high.

Feliz stepped in close, dug the muzzle of his pistol into Bishop's crotch, and pulled Bishop's phone and gun off him. "Come with me, *Special* Agent Bishop."

Chapter Twenty-Seven

Wynn shut the door behind her, double-locked it, and leaned against it, closing her eyes. Her memory frightened her, but she thought again of last night: the scuffle, the blood. Look at it again, she told herself. The noise, the scuffle...

Her eyes snapped open.

She was looking at the wrong thing.

What she should have been trying to see was the person who hit Pablo. Who was it that dealt the blow? Clearly, it had occurred in Pablo's room.

Crossing to the desk, she pulled a tooled-leather notebook from the drawer. On the front, stamped into the leather, were the words *Servicios para los Invitados*. Well, she mused, I'm an *invitado* if there ever was one, a repeat customer, and I need some *servicios*. Opening the book, she scanned through the tabs on the pages, considering the possibilities.

Check-in? No, the man who visited Pablo probably wasn't a guest. He'd be someone Pablo came to do business with.

Dining? No. Pablo had fallen from his balcony.

Room Service, then? Possibly, but how would that lead her to the identity of a guest in Pablo's room?

Turn-down Service, though. That had promise. She closed the book and picked up the *bulto* from Pablo's room, comparing it to the wood arm. The *bulto* was not as finely carved as the shard of arm, and yet the man in the gift shop had said it came from Arco Viejo.

She checked her watch. Aside from a cup of coffee with Feliz this morning, she'd had nothing since yesterday morning, and she was famished. She grabbed her purse and headed downstairs.

Crossing the lobby, she spotted Eliu Colón restocking newspapers. "Pardon me, *Señor* Colón," she began. "I need some information."

"I do not know what I can say to you," Colón said. He lifted the previous day's papers out of a rack and dropped them on the floor, narrowly missing her feet.

She looked down at yesterday's *New Mexican*, its headline reading, "Second Brutal Killing at Area Hotel."

"Look. My husband is in jail—"

"This, I know."

"I know you think I am not a good wife—"

Colón snorted.

Actually snorted, she thought, *out loud*. "My husband is in trouble, and I want to help him."

Dusting off his hands, Colón picked up a copy of the current day's newspaper and studied its headline: "Suspected Serial Killer Has Area on Edge." He dropped the paper on top of the pile, pushed past her, and stepped behind the desk. "And why do you come to me?"

This was not going well. She needed Colón on her side. "The thing is, I did some looking around on my own, and I think I found a clue."

"A clue?"

"A link. Something that will lead us to the real killer of *Señor* Estrella."

"But your husband—"

"The *bultos* in the gift shop," she said. "I understand most of those come from Arco Viejo."

Chapter Twenty-Eight

Driving County Road 309 after dark was reckless enough for a gringo but crazier still, Neron Diaz knew, for a half-drunk *buey loco* in a gold Corvette. Several miles east of Santa Fe, he took a right off the highway onto a road that stretched across an empty desert. He felt beneath the seat, pulled out his old Obregon pistol, flipped off the safety, and pulled back the slide.

The rear wheels of the car slipped sideways on the heavily-rutted road. Steering into the skid, Diaz dropped the gun, its barrel flashing as a shot blew into the passenger side door.

"*¡Puta!*" Diaz swore.

The car fishtailed again. He slapped at a late-season mosquito on his ankle and tapped the gas pedal, urging the roadster forward out of a pothole and across the scrub brush mesa. Ahead he could see the trailers and outbuildings that circled Arco Viejo like covered wagons.

He knew the villagers had not been happy to see Los Sapos set up shop in Arco Viejo nine years ago. They cooperated only because they knew the gang could rain a shitstorm on them if they did not. Instead, they took wicked delight in making Diaz's life a misery.

He'd hated every minute of the last year. He viewed living in Arco Viejo as doing time, sentenced to a bug-ridden, rundown apartment overlooking a manure yard, forced to listen to nothing but quiet because there was no television reception, not even on a dish, and not a whiff of nightlife. All he did was cope with the pigheaded carvers who tried, almost daily, to mess up his car.

He couldn't figure whether El Eché had sent him out here to do penance for something he'd no doubt done under the influence of mezcal, to test his loyalty to Los Sapos, or perhaps to demonstrate to the rest of the gang that he was a trusted soldier. Whichever it was, Diaz couldn't wait for the occasional weekends he spent in Santa Fe or, better yet, in Albuquerque. Every once in a while, he needed the club scene, a decent-looking woman, and a good meal.

He gunned the engine, the car's tires squealing as they bit on the cobblestones of the plaza. To his right, three *ancianas* crowded together in the moon shadow of the church, their arthritic old hands clutching at black headscarves. Left, in front of the tavern, a knot of young men stopped talking long enough to cast resentful eyes on Diaz and his gold Corvette. Whispering among themselves, they retreated inside the bar.

Diaz put the 'Vette in neutral, cut the headlights, and rolled silently downhill to a small warehouse where two trucks had parked, loaded with pallets of eight-by-eight pine timbers. He braked and smiled. Good. The shipment had come. Five workers unloaded the timbers, moving them hand to hand from the dock, up the hill to the doors of the warehouse. He heard the hum of the buzz saw and nodded, satisfied. Work would begin tonight.

He grabbed the Obregon off the floor and reset the safety. Climbing out of the car, he stuck the gun in his waistband and glanced in a window on the side of the building. Ignacio Garza's men sat at the table, one reading a newspaper while two others whittled. Garza stood with *Padré* Hernandez in the center of the room, watching all that went on.

Diaz resented the priest's constant presence. The man acted as though he, not Diaz, was the one in charge. Did that kind of arrogance come from all those years of leading a flock?

The priest's presence stunted Diaz's management style—with the *padré* standing there, he couldn't be as influential as he might be should a situation warrant persuasion. These men had little enough respect for him without the damned priest always around, ready to curb whatever coercion Diaz needed to exert.

The men hated him. Didn't take him seriously. He'd seen them roll their

CHAPTER TWENTY-EIGHT

eyes at his demands and make the jack-off move behind his back. They snickered when he suggested how they might take shortcuts in their work. The very thought of their disrespect pissed him off. He slapped at his ankle again, dispatching another mosquito. He would remind Ignacio—and the priest and the rest of them—who was boss. They needed a dose of his *mano duro*—and no one could hard-hand those crybabies like he could.

He pulled the gun from his waistband and threw the door open.

Chapter Twenty-Nine

Pumping Eliu Colón for information had been a dismal failure. Wynn grabbed a small pad from an alcove that enclosed a house phone and went to the dining room.

Once seated, she jotted: *Get numbers off Pablo's cell phone?* Good idea, probably impossible. She had no clue where his cell phone was at this point—the police had it, most likely, or it was at the mortuary in his shirt pocket. But with Phillip in custody, the police might not think to check Pablo's cell phone for leads on other suspects. They wouldn't want new facts to confuse what they believed was a closed case.

How else could she find out who the mystery man was?

She wrote again: *Fingerprints from Pablo's room?* What was she thinking? Did this come from watching too much TV? Even if she could lift a fingerprint, only the police would have a database to look it up in.

Did the killer bring the bulto that I found on Pablo's shelf? Maybe it was the guy in the gift shop? There was no way of knowing how the *bulto* got into Pablo's room. And, of course, it wasn't the guy from the gift shop—Feliz had already told her that man was dead too. Killed in the same way Pablo had been. The *bulto* would have all kinds of fingerprints on it, from her own and Pablo's to those of the carver from Varco Alejo… Arco Viejo…wherever…

She gave her head a quick shake. It was always worse when she was tired. She'd hardly slept the night before, and somehow she thought she could solve a murder?

She signaled the waiter for her check. Phillip would be all right for another few hours, and now that she'd eaten, she thought she could sleep.

CHAPTER TWENTY-NINE

* * *

Ordierno Feliz said nothing as he drove back to the police station with FBI Agent André Bishop in the passenger seat.

Of course Wynn Cabot was capable of murder, he decided. She clearly did not think as other women thought—her husband said so. And, after all, had she not cut off his advance? Who in her position, given the chance, would be foolish enough to refuse the attentions of a sheriff? All it would have taken was a kiss, and perhaps a bit more, to convince him of her innocence. Well, innocent of murder, at least. No, he knew she was not wholly innocent. A woman who would cheat on a wealthy husband? *Ella esta loca*—he had other ways to make her confess, and though he hesitated to use husbands against wives, he imagined that an angry Phillip Cabot could be a mighty force.

He parked and scrolled through his phone messages—would women never stop calling him? Grabbing Bishop out of the car by the back of his jacket, he marched the FBI agent in the back door of the courthouse, his pistol pushed as far into Bishop's ass as he could dig. The two of them went down the back stairway into the basement.

Wynn glanced down once more at the pool and then drew the curtains against the late-morning sun that glared back at her. She kicked off her sandals and stared at the house phone, willing it to ring, wondering if it would, and, if it did, who might be calling. Then her ears closed against the sounds of the hotel around her. She stretched out on the bed, pulled an extra pillow under her head, and gave herself up to oblivion.

She roused only once during her nap, thinking of lights—pool lights, bar room lights, headlights.

And then a muggy Houston summer afternoon surrounded her. Lace curtains blew at the window; a rocking chair moved in the breeze. She tasted beer on her tongue and descended a flight of stairs to a basement, where she saw a workbench arrayed with claw hammers and hooks. Above the workbench, a noose swung from the rafters. Outside again, a thunderstorm blew up, obliterating the sunny afternoon. She stood still, hypnotized by the wind, and a chess board blew off the patio table, scattering its game pieces into the yard.

The storm intensified, turning day into night, and she found herself at a party, talking. The party ended late, it seemed, near four in the morning, and she took her handbag and walked out to the deep end of Vista Cielo's pool. Next thing she knew, someone pulled her from a river. She turned into a monarch butterfly and flew away.

Wynn awoke as though rising from the bottom of a deep pool: coming up slowly, breaking the surface of wakefulness, dipping back into sleep again, surfacing once more to inhale air into her lungs and open her eyes. Swimming through the heap of pillows toward the nightstand, she looked at the clock: 7:30 PM. She'd slept all day.

As she walked into the restaurant, the room fell silent. Stares followed her as the hostess showed her to a table, where she hesitated before she sat. If she turned her back to the crowd, she'd face the balconies; the other direction, she'd be looking at the crowd in the dining room. She chose to face the room—it was still too difficult to stare at Pablo's balcony.

A waiter approached. *"Hola, senora*—long day, *que no?"*

Once again, she tried to shake off the grogginess. "You know what happened?"

The waiter shrugged. "Everyone knows what happened. All the staff knows, and I think all the guests, too."

"Yes, looks like. Tell you what...what is your name?"

"Jorgé."

"Okay, tell you what, Jorgé, I'd like a mojito and some information."

"Si?"

"Did anyone on the staff see someone—a man, probably—visit *Señor* Estrella last night?"

"I'll ask around, but first, I bring your mojito."

Wynn's dinner dragged, each mouthful difficult for her to swallow in front of an audience. She sipped at her mojito, smiling and waving at those who stared until they looked away.

CHAPTER TWENTY-NINE

When Jorge brought a flan and the check, he hesitated. "I am sorry, *Señora*. No one on the dining staff saw *Señor* Estrella's guest." He leaned in. "But I suggest you ask the valet."

Of course, she thought. Hastily, she scrawled her name across the dinner check and ran from the table, her rapid departure giving diners something new to whisper about over coffee.

The valet stepped in front of her. In the light of torches that framed the entry his teeth shone impossibly white against his tanned skin as he smiled. "I am sorry, *Señora*. Sheriff. Feliz says you do not leave the hotel."

"I'm not going anywhere. I want to talk to you."

He pointed to himself.

"Yes, you," she snapped. "I want to know who came to see *Señor* Estrella last night."

The valet looked into the lobby of the resort, his smile gone, his Adam's apple bobbing up and down as he swallowed nervously. Taking her arm, he pulled her out of the line of sight of the reception desk. "Please," he whispered. "I know the man who visited *Señor* Estrella, but he...I cannot tell you who he was."

"But I need to know. My husband is in jail, and I think this man—"

"Everyone wishes they could help," the valet said. "But this man is very powerful in the town we come from. We are afraid for our families that live out there."

"What town?" she asked, even though she knew the answer.

Chapter Thirty

Near dawn, the pitch of a scream wakened Nerón Diaz from a sound sleep. He bounded from his bed, slipped into his *huaraches*—out here, the damned scorpions would chew your toes off, given the chance—and ran to the window.

Decorations for tomorrow's *Dia de los Muertos* dangled half-finished from the buildings around the square—flower chains draped from balconies, towers of multi-colored ribbons awaiting their stands leaned against the buildings like sleepy drunks, the cottonwood pile for the bonfire built ten feet high.

An *anciana*, her black dress flapping behind her, ran toward the wood shop carrying a bundle of white rags, Father Hernandez at her heels in his black cassock, his morning mass interrupted by emergency.

Vultures flying to the carrion, Diaz thought. What the fuck had happened?

He pulled on a shirt and a pair of shorts and took the flight of stairs two at a time down to the street, glancing briefly at his Corvette as he turned toward the shop.

What the…had he seen what he thought he'd seen, or did the light of dawn play tricks? Was that a damned snake on the hood of his car? These fucking people—they would pay before he left town.

Villagers crowded around a pale Ignacio Garza, who sat at his work table, his carving hand elevated above his head, wrapped in a blood-soaked rag. Diaz gasped at the sight. His most valuable craftsman, injured. Did this mean work would have to stop? And if so, how many pieces had the men finished?

Last night, after he'd made them understand, for the umpteenth time, who

CHAPTER THIRTY

was boss around here, he'd asked for seventy *bultos*. A mere seventy—was that so many? He'd given them until this afternoon to finish, showing that he could be a reasonable man. Each of them, then, would be responsible for ten carvings, though he knew the pious Ignacio would be slow, taking pains to make his *bultos* as artistic as he could.

Artistic, feh. Fuck artistic. People didn't buy art any more. When they bought a *santo* they bought what they *thought* was a slice of New Mexican folklore. It made not a whiff of difference to tourists whether the thing had finely carved fingernails or how divine was the expression on the face—in fact, the more rustic, the better, so far as gringos were concerned.

"What is it, Ignaz? Where are you cut?" Diaz asked.

Garza pointed to the fleshy spot between his thumb and index finger. The worst. It meant the *santero* might not be able to grip a chisel for weeks, if ever again.

Diaz pounded the work table. "*Estupido!*" He pulled a knife from where it was lodged on the tabletop and stabbed into the table once, twice, four times, six, before he stopped. "*Me cago in la leche!*"

The priest stepped forward, his fists clenched. "This is not your bad luck, Nerón. Ignacio has lost far more than a day's worth of work, which is all you have lost. This might not have happened if you did not push these men to work without sleep."

A general murmur of assent went up from the men around the table.

Diaz looked at his workers. "And how many *bultos* are done?"

The men fell silent.

"How many?"

A small *santero* named Manny spoke. "Nine carved and painted, *Señor* Diaz, six more carved but not yet sanded and colored. Fifteen in all, if we finish those." He shrugged. "*Dios de los Muertos* begins tomorrow—we will not be working then."

Diaz's face flushed. "You will work until I tell you to stop working, Manny. That includes feast days if I need the work done then, do you understand?"

"*Bastardo,*" someone mumbled from the back of the crowd.

Diaz held out a hand. That remark had made his mind up for him. "Let me see."

Manny plucked a *bulto* replica from those at the end of the work table and handed it to Diaz for his inspection. Diaz compared the original against the copy. The crude copy looked as though it had been carved and painted by a five-year-old, its green paint slopped over the ends of the robe onto the hands and feet of the statue. He upended the copy, checking underneath, and then threw the figure against the wall, breaking off the arms and head. "This is not what I asked for. These are hideous, and the cavity inside is too small."

Manny winced. "Perhaps if you could tell us the purpose of the cavity we could—"

Diaz grabbed the *santero* by his chin and shoved him against the wall. "You do not need to know the purpose of the cavity, Manuelito. All you need to do is your job. None of you has finished your quota of *bultos*, have you?" Diaz looked around at the men. *"Have you?"*

"Nerón, the men are exhausted," Father Hernandez said. "It is, no doubt, the reason Ignacio's chisel slipped...."

Diaz clenched his teeth and tried to restrain himself from hitting the priest. "Pack up what is here, Manny."

The *santero* pulled a box from under the table and packed the few finished pieces. Diaz tossed the broken San Lorenzo on top of the lot. "Even though it is a long and dangerous ride, I will take these to a shop in Santa Fe, and all of you had better pray I sell them," he said. "Or we will celebrate more dead tomorrow than we'd planned to."

He jerked a thumb in the direction of the gold Corvette. "Put the box on the passenger seat of my car—and while you're there, *get the fucking rattlesnake off the hood."*

Christ, Diaz thought, it was dry as Death Valley out here. He could use a drink. He stood over Ignacio Garza, watching the village *curandero* stitch and bandage the deep cut in Garza's right hand. A small crowd of *santeros* and *ancianas* had gathered around, grumbling about the hours they worked, the unsafe conditions. Diaz chuckled to himself—the villagers were so bored they'd watch anything. "Do not worry, *mi compadre*," Diaz said to Garza. "You

CHAPTER THIRTY

will be good as new in no time."

The healer squinted up at Diaz. "Do not worry? Good as new? How easy for you to say, Diaz. This is not your hand. This hand will take many months to heal. Ignacio will not be able to carve for a year or more, that I can tell you. Perhaps not ever again."

"It is as though you have cut off my hand, Diaz," Garza wailed.

The crowd murmured. Diaz heard "Damn right," and, "No more working for a bully," and, "That does it."

Diaz rolled his eyes. These people could get worked up over nothing. "I'll take care of you, Ignacio," Diaz assured him. "Your family should not be troubled. Think of this as a well-earned vacation, *si*? Can you do that?"

Pain shot up his arm as Ignacio Garza watched Nerón Diaz pull away from the plaza in his metal-flake gold car. The slice in Garza's hand extended from below his wrist, where the chisel had first dug in, deep through the big muscle in his thumb. After the *curandero* got the bleeding stopped—and there had been a lot of blood—he had slathered the cut with the *zabila* from an aloe plant and took eighteen stitches to close the wound. He had told Garza he needed to go to the hospital in Santa Fe, but that was not possible, even though his hand throbbed like a *tambora*.

Garza called his *santeros* together. "*Mi amigos*," he began and winced in pain as he held up a large, intricately carved *bulto*. "It is fitting that earlier this week, for the feast of Saint Jude, I should carve my last fine piece, a *santo* of our *patrón* of desperate causes." He lowered the statue, newly bloody from his wound.

The men waited.

"We need to leave Arco Viejo, my brothers," Garza continued. "When Nerón Diaz returns, I fear for our families and for your lives. I do not think Diaz will come back alone. He will have men from Los Sapos with him, I suspect. And perhaps many guns."

Diaz knew the moment he saw the length and depth of the cut in Ignacio's hand that the Arco Viejo project had been scuttled. The difference between fifteen—now fourteen—*bultos* and the seventy he had demanded meant a half-million-dollar difference to Los Sapos. When El Eché heard about the accident, he would be furious. Diaz did not exactly know the extent of El Eché's fury, having never met the man—no one had ever met him—but stories of his rages were legend. Going back to Veracruz, lying in a hammock drinking *pulche* had become a distant dream with the slip of Ignacio's chisel.

He wondered if Ignacio had cut himself on purpose, to spite him. He wondered what Los Sapos would do when they heard that their strategy for moving the gold had fizzled. He wondered if he would live through the consequences.

He supposed he could use Manny and the other *santeros* to carve the statues, but it was Ignacio who finished the pieces well enough that they got decent money from the collectors and museums. There was still the possibility that they could move the gold in *bultos* that weren't carved and painted so well, but they would have to find avenues for marketing them other than through the high-end auction houses such as Sotheby's and Christie's.

His only hope of living, so far as he could tell, would be to contrive some way of moving the gold and selling it into a legal market. That would be the only thing that concerned Los Sapos and, he suspected, the cartel's man in the U.S.—El Eché himself.

Chapter Thirty-One

Holding the phone in his left hand, Nerón Diaz steered with his elbow while he downshifted, clipping branches off the scrub pine and chamisa as he drove. He jerked the wheel to dodge another pothole and corrected just in time to miss an oncoming car.

"What do you mean, 'We have only a few more coming'?" El Eché's voice grew soft and low—the sound of distant thunder. He was building to one of his rages.

Diaz gulped. "I am sorry, Eché, but I mean just that. Garza's days as a *santero* are finished. The rest of them turn out work that looks like it was done with a chain-saw."

"We can't sell those, you idiot—Vista Cielo already has too much shoddy crap in its gift shop. You've made a mess out there."

"But this was not my fault," Diaz whined, switching ears. Why did everyone call him an idiot? He was smarter than they knew—of course he was. Wasn't that why El Eché appointed him to run the Arco Viejo operation in the first place? "Why do you think I'm telling you this, Eché? Jack up the prices on the pieces Ignacio Garza has already done—they are collectors' items. These statues just became rare."

El Eché went silent. Diaz looked at his phone. Eché had hung up on him.

He swerved again, narrowly missing a pothole the size of a casket. There was too much traffic out here for such a narrow road—all the tourists returning to Vista Cielo after shooting the Rio Grande's hellacious rapids or touring the ruins at Pecos.

Diaz threw his phone on the seat and gripped the steering wheel with both hands. Damn this road. He hated this drive, especially in this kind of light: the smoldering fog of a late autumn dawn, when everything looked larger than life—the desert, the potholes, the…Diaz squinted into the hazy light, struggling to make sense of a shape on his windshield.

What *was* that? A sudden spot of mud? A leaf?

Oh, Jesus save me, Diaz prayed, trembling at the sight of a giant tarantula.

He slammed on the brakes, the back end of the Corvette fishtailing to a stop. God damn, he thought, still shaking as he steered the car to the side of the road and cut the engine. Staring at the furry black body as big as the palm of his hand, he flipped the windshield wipers. Take that, *trozo de mierda*, he thought, watching the creature fly off to the side of the road.

He pulled a pint of tequila from the console, twisted off the lid, and emptied half down his throat. There, he thought, his hands steadier. That's better. He watched the tarantula hobble along the shoulder of the road, stopping at the driver's side door of the car.

Diaz looked down at the spider, the early-morning shot of tequila burning in his otherwise empty stomach. Slowly, he reached across, his hand still trembling, and locked the door. Then he remembered. Tonight was *La Noche de las Brujas*. The night of the witches. Halloween. Everyone would be jumpy today.

He chuckled at his own foolishness and pushed the ignition button to start the car. The engine coughed but did not turn over. Flooded, he thought. Shit. Halfway to the main highway, *la mala luna*—the evil moon—setting over the mesa and a giant tarantula waiting for him to get out. Shit. Shit, shit, shit.

"*Hijo de puta*," came a voice from behind him.

Diaz froze. The voice sounded as though it was in the car. He closed his eyes, hoping this was all a bad dream.

"You, Diaz," the voice wheezed, close behind.

Yes, the voice was definitely in the car, he decided. And certainly from the back, where his shotgun lay. His Obregon pistol was in the glove compartment, out of ammunition. He lifted his head and opened one eye, peering into the rearview mirror. Out of the black, he could discern a man's face, blood dripping from a wound on his head, his dark hair slicked straight

CHAPTER THIRTY-ONE

back to reveal a star-shaped birthmark on his right temple.

"Look," Pablo Estrella's voice whispered. "Out there."

Again Diaz squinted into the foggy distance, barely able to make out something that rolled and bobbed along the highway. Something small. Round. Nothing to be afraid of, he decided. Probably an armadillo—it looked hairless—and...and...recoiling from the image rolling toward him, Diaz buried his face in his hands. "Jesus." He spread his fingers, peering again at the disembodied human head as it bounced closer—the head of...he looked again, not wanting to believe what he'd first seen.

"Oh, God, no," Diaz wailed as his own head rolled by. "It's me!"

Chapter Thirty-Two

Shortly after room service delivered her breakfast, Wynn sat on the balcony of the second-floor room Feliz had assigned her. In one sense, she loathed being that far from the comfort of the pool; in another, she appreciated the distance she had from the site where she'd found Pablo.

She held the San José she'd taken from Pablo's room in her left hand, trying to get a feel for the piece, to see if she could sense the artisanship that went into it. The carving of the hair was smooth and graceful, as were the folds in the robe. And yet the carving was cruder, rougher, more hastily executed than the arm piece she'd found on the floor of Pablo's room.

She held the carving close to her cheek and closed her eyes, sensing, smelling, listening to it, and then set it on the patio table and stood, intending to look at the San José from above. But what was she seeing? She turned and frowned. The *bulto* didn't sit on the table so much as it floated an eighth of an inch above it. Taking it up again, she tipped the San José over to examine its base, afraid she'd find evidence that the piece was turned on a lathe to take off excess wood the easy way, so the carving would be less arduous.

What she discovered instead was that the bottom had a plug of wood fitted into it, a block set into a square hole. The block did not fit exactly, but protruded so that when the statue was placed on a flat surface, the base did not sit entirely flush.

I don't know why that would be, she thought, but it looks pretty cool, visually. Still, a good *bulto* should sit firmly on its base.

Carrying the statue into the room, she took a fork from her breakfast tray

CHAPTER THIRTY-TWO

and tried to force the tines into the opening cut around the block, but the tines were too wide to pry out the block. The tightly jammed block of wood didn't budge.

More hasty work by a carver, she thought. Exchanging the fork for a table knife, she worked its blade into the crack and then around the perimeter, turning the knife sideways until the block backed out part way. Splintering the wood, she grappled and pulled until the block dislodged to reveal a small recess inside the *bulto*, roughly two inches square and equally deep.

Her dyslexia kicked in and, like a camera taking rapid exposures, she mentally recorded the image from all angles. Jerking her head up, she felt the room spin. She groped for a chair and sat, fighting to calm herself. What is this for? Why is it here? She'd never seen a recess carved into a base of a *bulto* before.

She studied the hollow inside again—a cavity slightly larger than her cupped palm, a smooth deep recess. Large enough to hold—what? A ring? A few coins? Were these being sold to people who wanted to hide valuables from burglars, like the fake soft drink cans and toothpaste tubes?

But no, she thought, if someone wanted to hide things, they'd need more room even than this to bootleg something past customs and into another country. Maybe it was just for the *santero*, the carver, to smuggle messages out of Arco Viejo? Were they using the statues to get messages out of Arco Viejo to someone here at Vista Cielo. The statues came here, the messages were delivered, and the *bulto* could be sold in the gift shop. But what message was so secret someone had to go to this length to deliver it? What message was important enough to kill for?

Seamus Caine switched his phone to his newly-manicured left hand, leaned back in his chair, and sighed as the manicurist pulled one of his feet up into her lap.

"But the problem I have to solve," Wynn said, "is how to clear myself so I can get out of here and go home."

"Where are the police on this?"

"They've virtually tried and convicted Phillip. But I found something when

I was looking at the *bultos*. They have false bottoms."

"False what?"

"They have these—I don't know, big plugs in the bottoms of them. Like a piggy bank. When you pull the plug out, there's a hollow cavity inside."

Caine frowned, drumming manicured fingers on his belly while he thought. "Most peculiar. Highly, highly irregular. Never heard of *santeros* doing that."

"Nor I. Then I remembered the valet saying that the town where these come from is being terrorized by the man who was with Pablo the night he was murdered. I think the *santeros* are sending something to their people on the outside, something concealed in the *bultos*."

"And I think your imagination is hyperactive."

"I need to go back to Arco Viejo. I have to prove my innocence, Seamus, and Phillip's. And by the way, your boy Bishop isn't doing anything to help us—I can't even reach him these days."

"Wynn, darling, this could be foolish. I'm sure Bishop is out of touch because he's working on the mysterious appearances of the Zuni San Gabriel. That is, after all, the only reason he's out there. He has no jurisdiction over a murder case, remember."

"Listen, if you don't hear from me again by morning, call the Cruz County jail and tell Sheriff Feliz that he can find my body somewhere in Arco Viejo."

Wynn left Caine listening to a dead line. Damn that girl, he thought, she could be as maddening as any child.

He dismissed his manicurist and lay back on the bank of pillows arrayed three deep at the head of his king-sized bed. He glanced at the clock—a few minutes before four in the afternoon. Nearly ten o'clock at night in France. Almost bedtime. He thought about his apartment in Marseilles overlooking rue Edmond Rostand, the narrow street that ran outside his window in the sixth *arrondissement*, in the *Quartier des Antiquaries*. He closed his eyes and began to float toward a patisserie he knew all too well, smelling the duck confit at his favorite bistro, walking summer street markets held on the occasional Sunday…stalls of odd jewelry and bric-a-brac and old military maps…

He sighed. Who was he kidding? He wasn't going to sleep while Wynn was

CHAPTER THIRTY-TWO

in trouble two thousand miles away. He threw back the duvet and swung his feet to the floor. Alice jumped down from the bed and yelped as though she, too, understood trouble was in the air. Caine walked to the far side of the bed, grabbed up his phone, and paused. Was it time to call the man who could get *anyone* out of a jam? He found the number he wanted and texted a message.

Chapter Thirty-Three

Sunrise colored the sky behind the cathedral as a black Lincoln Town Car rolled through the quiet streets of Arco Viejo's courthouse square. Phillip Cabot sat in the back seat next to an attorney from a local firm.

"I don't do much work out here," the attorney said. "Few folks out here have enough money to hire me. And after seeing what I saw this morning, I'm not sure I want to practice much law in Cruz County."

Cabot snorted a laugh. "Damned shame, isn't it? Someone of your talents, someone who can make that midget sweat? I like that in a man." He didn't give a Texas two-step how much more fortunate he was than other poor bastards who didn't have the coin to muster out of the Cruz County jail. He needed a steak, a drink, and a decent night's sleep.

The car slowed to enter the driveway at Vista Cielo and stopped in front of the entrance.

"Here you are, Mr. Cabot," the attorney said. "I'll send my bill directly to Tripp Tripplehorn." He caught Cabot's sleeve. "A free word of advice, sir. Watch your ass, because I guaran-damn-tee you Feliz will be watching it. It would be a good idea if you and your wife left New Mexico, and pronto. We appreciate your business, but I don't relish the idea of going to court on your behalf. The writ worked this time—next time, they may find evidence."

Cabot chuckled. "So you really think I killed Pablo Estrella?"

The attorney raised an eyebrow. "What I think doesn't matter as much as what the cops might cook up to convict you. I've dealt with Feliz's kind before. When he has to release someone he wants the world to believe is

CHAPTER THIRTY-THREE

guilty, he isn't happy. He's likely to arrest you again for… Well, just about anything. Shouting in public, for example, or throwing fireworks." The attorney shrugged. "You run the risk is all I'm saying. As long as you're in town. So scram, Mr. Cabot. *Vamanos.* You're fortunate everything they had was circumstantial, and Feliz wasn't quick enough to plant evidence—that little son of a bitch didn't have anything concrete that pointed to you. This time."

"We'll see. The wife and I booked for ten days, and we've still got a few days left to honeymoon."

Cabot looked out the back window, then at the entrance, expectantly. "I reckon nobody's around to open a car door this early," he said, opening the door himself. "Christ on a cracker, can't even get good help if you pay for it, apparently."

He stood and then leaned back into the car. "By the way, there's a kid over in that jail named Alberto—he's diabetic, and he's in bad shape. Feliz won't feed him until he gives up what he was doing with a bunch of syringes. Go bail him out and add it to my bill."

"I'll do what I can, Cabot. Remember what I told you."

Cabot knocked twice on the roof of the car. "Thanks, Calderón," he called. *"Muchas gracias."*

He sighed as he watched the Lincoln glide down the drive and out onto the highway. Feliz had been mad as a bull in the bumblebees when Calderón showed up, waving a writ of habeas corpus. What a scene that had been: Feliz strutting around gobbling like a turkey, his chest puffed out, feathers ruffled, pecking at Cabot while he still could. Picking, niggling, digging at him until Calderón hustled him to the car, and not a moment too soon. Another five minutes of that little shit, Cabot thought, and I'd have been back in Feliz's hoosegow for assault and battery on a sheriff.

He pushed into the hotel room, went immediately to the bathroom, stripped to his underwear, and turned on the shower. When he came back into the bedroom, there stood Wynn, holding a *bulto*. He threw up his hands and backed away. "Whoa—it's me, Hon, back from the hoosegow."

Wynn started in his direction. "Phillip…look what I—"

"Hon, believe me. You don't want to get close to me just yet—I'm a breeding ground for fleas and bed bugs. Really—I need a shower before I kiss you hello." He stared at her for a moment. "You Okay?"

"Alive. Been better, but sure. Why do you ask?"

"Well, let's see. Guys are getting killed all around us, I've been forty-eight hours in the slammer…I dunno, just a thought."

"I'm under house arrest, Agent Bishop has taken a powder, and you want to know, am I fine?"

"You need to cut back a notch," Cabot said, turning for the bathroom. "I just did time for you. That's where I've been. Proving my love by taking one for the team."

He locked the bathroom door and emerged half an hour later, showered and shaved, a towel wrapped around his waist. "Got the key to the mini-bar? I could use a jolt."

"Not right now," she said. "Look at this." She held up the plug from the bulto and its base. "This has something to do with the murders, I think. It's hollowed out and plugged. It might mean something that could clear us."

"Uh huh, fascinating. And that would be 'clear you' since I'm on my way out of here. But first, we need to talk."

"We couldn't talk when you first showed up?"

"Well, I…"

She stared at him. "What? Talk."

"Calderón, the attorney Tripp sent to spring me, thinks we should leave town. That we should get as far away from here as we can get and as soon as we can. He suggested Illinois. His words. Can you imagine? 'Maybe go to fuckin' Illinois,' he said." Cabot paused. "Frankly, Hon, Feliz likes you for the murder of the guy downstairs. The one in the gift shop. He was killed the same way your friend was. But Feliz ain't got nothin', really. If we want to go, we go."

Wynn took a deep breath. 'Killed the same way your friend was.' There was only one way Phillip could know that—Feliz must have told him. And she thought she knew why. "So you do a two-day turn in jail, and things between us are hunky-dory again?"

CHAPTER THIRTY-THREE

"No, I do not think things are hunky-dory at all, Hon." Cabot hauled out a suitcase and began to pack. "I think you were catting around on me with your buddy Pablo there before you ever moved out of the house. Or should I say your *late* buddy. Ex-friend. *Deceased lover.*" He took her by the shoulders. "How long had that been going on?"

She shook loose of his grasp. "Let me understand this—I told you how many times that unless you paid me some attention, that unless we went out once in a while, that if you didn't start coming home at a decent hour *and staying there* so we could have something that resembled a marriage—"

"Yeah, yeah. You'd go out and find someone who would. Well, whoop-de-do. You did it. Then something blew up between you two, and you killed him." Cabot threw shirts on top of the pile of golf shorts and underwear.

Wynn fought for a breath. "I didn't meet him until after I moved out of your house, *and I didn't kill him.*" She hated arguments like this one—they spent all her energy, and none of what she ever said felt good.

"And the guy in the gift shop? Seems there was a room charge wadded in his hand when they found him—and it had your signature on it. If you didn't kill those men, who did?"

"I don't know who did."

Cabot pulled the separation agreement out of his suitcase and threw it on the bed. "That's for you." He snapped the suitcase's latches shut and walked to the door. "'Bye, Hon. I'm outta here like I stole something."

Wynn watched the door shut and then snatched the document up off the bed. She scanned the first page and realized what he'd done—Phillip had known all the time he was here that, eventually, he would give her the separation she'd asked for more than a year ago. "You did steal something," she murmured. "You stole my heart, and I want it back."

Once again, Bishop's cell phone rolled to voice mail, and once again, Wynn left a message. Where had he gone? He hadn't said he was leaving town—she was pretty sure he would've told her. As little as she knew him, she thought he would stick around to be sure Feliz didn't harass her. And then an odd, and oddly liberating, feeling came over her: she was alone—Caine was too far away to be any real help, she couldn't reach Bishop, Phillip had gone who knew where, and Pablo... gone for good.

Feliz waited for fifteen minutes after he saw Cabot leave the room, suitcase in hand, then stepped to the door. Just seeing her again would keep his anger alive. He knocked and closed his eyes, letting bile warm his blood and stoke the rage in his brain. He craved the rush, let it guide his actions.

All the New Age apostles around here would tell him to let it go, he fumed, to keep from dirtying his soul. But he was a man who enjoyed robust feelings. Nothing could corrupt him.

Her husband had left, and rightly so. Why would any man who was really a man put up with such a wife? She whored behind his back. Never mind that Cabot did it too. A woman should not be so tempted. Estrella had come along, and—bam—she was on her back in a minute.

He knocked again. "Mrs. Cabot," he called, his voice shaking with anger. "Sheriff Feliz. Open the door, please." *Oh yes,* he thought. *Open the door, Mrs. Cabot, because I have plans for you.*

Chapter Thirty-Four

DaShaye Williams needed to recheck a part of the evidence in a car theft ring he'd been working—two guys stealing late model SUVs from in front of convenience stores and always—*but always*—Williams had arrived at the convenience stores just a few minutes too late to catch the perps. But late last night he'd arrested a pair of gangbangers selling drugs in front of the Albertsons and both of them had worn large rings of keys on their hips. He wanted to have another look at those keys.

Day before yesterday, for some reason, Feliz had declared the evidence lockers off-limits, but Feliz wasn't around—probably off "fundraising" again, Williams thought, or hanging around Vista Cielo, making life miserable for the Cabot woman. The hell with Feliz and his new rule about the evidence locker, Williams decided. He'd take a quick trip downstairs, have a look at the key rings, and be back at his desk before Feliz came in.

Rather than using the painfully slow hydraulic elevator, he took the back stairway down to the basement, walked toward the front of the building, to the cages where the evidence was kept locked case-by-case, lifted the sign-in clipboard from its nail, and paused. He listened. Traffic outside? Deputies moving chairs in the offices above? No, there was something else…something closer about the noise he heard.

He rehung the clipboard on its nail, unsnapped the strap on his holster, pulled out his flashlight, and moved to the dark corner beyond the cages.

The sound came again, this time louder.

Simultaneously Williams snapped on his flashlight and drew his gun. He jumped at what he saw. And he almost forgot to yell, "Freeze!"

DAY OF THE DEAD

* * *

"Sheriff," Wynn began, "I found something out about the *bultos*." She started for the closet, but Feliz grabbed her arm. She flinched. He gripped her forearm so tightly his fingernails dug into her skin.

He put his face close to hers, breathing her in. Such a beautiful woman. How irksome that her beauty could arouse him even more than she made him angry.

"Look," she said, pulling away from his grip, "the bases of these *bultos* are hollowed out—they're hollow. I think someone is using them to move something. Something they probably don't want anyone to find, until the right person comes to remove it. And I think that whatever that *something* is, it's what got Pablo Estrella killed."

"But what about our *compadré* here in the gift shop? How do you explain that? Are you the one who removes the…"—he circled his hands in midair—"the whatever it is, and when Estrella and this shop clerk found out about your scheme, you had to kill them? Doing what you do for a living would make smuggling very much easier, *qué no*, Mrs. Cabot? Are you trying to throw blame elsewhere because you are the one who is our smuggler?"

Wynn looked at him, incredulous. "No. I only just discovered the false bottoms on the pieces today."

Feliz rolled his eyes. "Ah. It took you this long to contrive a story, then? Your husband said it might. So how is it, please, that you didn't kill these men?"

"Look, we have to go to Arco Viejo." She held up the *bulto* for his inspection. "This piece was not crafted for the tourist market. It's of a better quality than that. But I have never seen one with a false bottom and a cavity big enough to hide…I don't know what. The *santero* who made this works in Arco Viejo. That's where we'll find our answers."

Feliz paused, astounded. Odd that she should say that. He had to go back to Arco Viejo himself this afternoon to talk to Father Hernandez. What *did*

CHAPTER THIRTY-FOUR

she know?

He nodded. So, it would go this way, would it? She had made a decision that might get her killed, but it would be her own fault. One less thing to worry about if he took her along. After all, she would not try to escape if she was going where she had asked to go. And it would certainly be easier on everyone if she died out there. No one would know where to look for her.

"Maybe you are right, Mrs. Cabot," he said. "As a practical matter, it would be easier to keep an eye on you if I take you to Arco Viejo myself, since you are determined to go. Perhaps we will discover more about what happened here at Vista Cielo, perhaps not." Once again, he took her by the arm, this time steering her out to the patrol car. "But you must ride in back."

DaShaye Williams gently pulled the duct tape away from Agent André Bishop's wrists. "You can pull the rest of the tape away—I don't want to hurt you. And I guess I don't need to ask who put you down here." He grimaced as Bishop yanked the tape off his mouth.

Bishop massaged the skin around his lips, peeling away small pieces of adhesive. "You'd get the answer you're expecting."

Williams helped Bishop to his feet. "Who are you?"

Bishop reached into his jacket and then sighed. "Feliz took my ID. I'm with the FBI—Agent André Bishop. With the Art Crimes unit. You can verify that with the New Mexico field office, or with the office in D.C."

"How long you been down here?"

"Long enough to need a meal and a shower."

"You do need a shower, that's for sure."

"What's today?"

"Yeah, it's, uh, Tuesday."

"Then two days—that little turd put me down here two days ago."

Williams nodded. That would fit. That would have been the day Feliz declared the evidence locker off-limits to everyone in the office but himself.

Bishop looked around the room. "Bastard took my phone, my ID, my..." he checked inside his jacket, "yeah, my pistol."

"Wait—how'd you get here?"

"Feliz hijacked me in the parking lot at my hotel. Stuck a gun in my ass and off we went. I need to get in touch with some folks—my office, a couple of others connected to a case I'm working. You got a prisoner here by the name of Cabot?"

"His attorney sprung him yesterday. We had nothing on him, really. Except Feliz didn't like him."

"I don't like him either, but I don't think he killed your guy at the hotel." Bishop pulled his plastic hotel key card from a hip pocket and held it up. "At least I can get to a shower, and after that, a sandwich. Let's go."

At the end of the bar, sitting in the same spot where Phillip Cabot had left him three days ago, the skinhead freak with the flaming skull tattoo was drunk as a beaver in a brewery, a row of Pacifico beer bottles lined up in front of him. Cabot slid onto a stool at the opposite end of the bar and waved down the bartender. The bartender poured two fingers of Gentleman Jack into a glass and slid it down the bar, the glass stopping tidily right in front of Cabot.

Cabot chuckled. "Thanks."

The bartender cocked his head and said, "Compliments of Mr. Diaz, there. Says he owes you one."

"He does," Cabot said, and drank.

Christ on a cracker, he thought. Had it been only five days since he'd arrived? This wasn't quite what he had in mind when he tuned up his nose for trouble. This trip had been a game-changer, but he no longer liked the game.

He'd thrown the separation agreement on the bed in a fit of pique. He wished he hadn't done that. Would definitely take that move back if he could. There was something—*something*—in him that loved a good argument with Wynn and a flourish at the end if it gave him the win. So what if his wife had had a lover?

Still, as he sipped his Gentleman Jack, a tiny voice deep within chirped like a cricket, *Good for her, good for her.*

No, Cabot thought. Not good for her. Not good for either one of us.

The voice argued, *But why shouldn't she?* and Cabot's mind argued back,

CHAPTER THIRTY-FOUR

Because I trusted her.

The voice squeaked again, *She trusted you, too, once. Until she found out what you were doing all those nights.*

That's different, Cabot thought. I'm a man. Men have needs. *And women should be held to a different standard?* his inner voice countered.

"Yes," Cabot said out loud. He couldn't finish the thought because he knew he'd hurt her, and repeatedly, but she'd tried to fix the marriage. Until she tired of trying. He hurt the same way she had hurt so many times, and he wasn't sure he could be as big about it as he'd asked her to be.

He felt like crying. His stomach churned, his head buzzed. He pushed his drink away, threw a twenty on the bar, and grabbed his suitcase.

"Mr. Cabot," the bartender yelled after him. "Do you want me to find you a new friend?"

"Not today, Pepe," Cabot shouted over his shoulder. "I have business to do."

He rounded the corner into the lobby in time to see Feliz hold open the back door of the patrol car for Wynn as she got in. He stopped and set down his suitcase, weighing his chances against the sheriff. This didn't seem like a good time to question Feliz's moves. The little bastard would use any opportunity to throw Cabot's ass back in jail, but where the hell were the two of them going? He and Feliz had an agreement for which he'd paid good money. Still, Wynn wasn't handcuffed. And she didn't look distraught.

Eliu Colón looked up from counting the cash drawer and glared at Cabot over the top of his reading glasses. "Mr. Cabot? Checking out?" Colón could not wait until this despicable couple left his hotel. Perhaps, since Cabot had a suitcase in hand, at least one of them was on his way.

Cabot pointed outside. "My wife. She...and Sheriff Feliz...?"

Colón nodded, giving Cabot an oily smile. "Yes. They just left. Mrs. Cabot is under house arrest, you'll recall. I believe, although I cannot be sure, that Sheriff Feliz is taking her to the jail."

"But, but I...he and I made a...I asked Feliz not to... Feliz told me he wouldn't take her there. I paid him..."

Frowning, Colón yanked off his glasses. "Do not suggest to me, Mr. Cabot, that you tried to bribe the sheriff of Cruz County."

Cabot shook his head. "No, of course not. I meant only that I paid him the highest praise for deciding Mrs. Cabot should not be taken to the jail. I am surprised that he changed his mind."

Colón cocked his head. "There is another chance...oh, but no. Probably not."

"What? If they didn't go to the jail, then...where?"

Colón leaned over the reception desk, motioning Cabot to lean in close. "Sheriff Feliz is quite the...*infatuate*." He leaned back and raised his eyebrows. "You know?"

"Quite the... what?"

Colón sighed, exasperated. Another hick Texan, expecting everyone to speak to him on his level. Not one of them could understand a nuanced remark. It was all words of one syllable for these people. "A lover boy, Mr. Cabot. Sheriff Feliz has a reputation, and he lives up to it. I would suggest that if he has not taken your wife to the jail, he has taken her to his apartment." There, Colón smiled to himself, that should, as they say in Texas, make him sweat like a virgin at a prison rodeo.

Cabot felt his stomach pitch. The damn bourbon was coming up. And then he felt a shift in his mood, as surely as though it was physical. His head cleared. His mid-life crisis dissipated. He still had legal problems, but he thought he knew how to save his marriage.

"A car," he gasped. "I need to rent a car."

Eliu Colón connected the phone call to the Cabot woman's room, knowing it would roll to voice mail since Mrs. Cabot had left not five minutes ago with Ordierno Feliz.

Bishop left a pleading message and sighed. He checked his watch and then dialed the number for Seamus Caine, knowing the phone call would awaken him.

Caine roused, frowned at his phone, not recognizing the number, and swiped the screen. "Anyone who calls at this hour, it better have to do with

CHAPTER THIRTY-FOUR

blood."

"This is André Bishop, Caine. And it might have to do with blood."

"Bishop, you know better than to—"

"I can't get hold of Wynn Cabot. I think she's in trouble."

"I think so, too, Bishop. And I told you not to let that happen."

"It's a long story, Seamus. I was kidnapped, but I'm loose, and I need to get to Wynn."

"Last time she and I talked, she said she needed to go back to Arco Viejo."

"Last time she and I talked, I told her not to leave the hotel—that she'd be better off with people around her. Everyone she meets out here is ending up dead."

Chapter Thirty-Five

Deputy Sheriff DaShaye Williams shook his head and stowed his phone in his pocket. He'd tried twice to raise Ordierno Feliz—he wasn't answering.

Twenty minutes ago, Williams and Bishop had arrived at the parking lot of the Budget Inn Express, where Bishop had left his car when Ordierno Feliz had kidnapped him two days before. The green government-issue Ford had vanished. While Bishop was inside cleaning up, Williams worked his cell phone.

"Hey," he said on his end of the conversation. "You get a green Ford with government tags on it in there in the last couple of days? No tags on it, huh? Mmm hmm. Anything come off it yet? Shit, really? *Really?*" He pounded a fist on the steering wheel and then raised an elbow as he held the phone to his ear again as Bishop got back in the car. Williams mouthed the words "Salvage yard. Engine block's gone." He looked out the car window again, staring at the spot where the Ford had sat. "No," he said into the phone, "I got the guy here that drives—drove—that car. Yeah. FBI. We'll sort that out later, but you shouldn't have taken Feliz's word on it. You know better."

Not half an hour after Ordierno Feliz pulled away from Vista Cielo, Agent Bishop and Deputy Williams pulled in. Williams parked squarely in front of the door, sauntered into the lobby, hiked up uniform pants laden with equipment, sniffed, and leaned his elbows on the hotel's front desk as though he was thinking.

Colón looked up over the top of his glasses. "Deputy?"

CHAPTER THIRTY-FIVE

"My boss here?"

"Left a while ago. Took Mrs. Cabot. Don't know where they're headed."

"Back into Arco Viejo, maybe?"

"Maybe. He didn't say."

Williams got back behind the wheel of the patrol car, reached for the button that blew the blues and twos, and then thought better of it. Feliz was somewhere in Arco Viejo with the Cabot woman—and it wouldn't take long to find out where. The town simply wasn't that big—he was there, or he wasn't.

If he wasn't, Williams thought he knew where he could find him. "We should have stayed out there, rather than chasing in here," he said to Bishop. "Feliz doesn't stand still for long." He pulled a business card from his pocket, scribbled a number on the back and handed it to Bishop. "Here. If we get separated, call me. I don't pick up if Feliz calls, but he doesn't have this number."

"I don't have a cell phone, remember?"

"Somebody will. You're a smart boy."

He and Bishop rode in companionable silence until Bishop said, "Cabot didn't kill that guy, you don't think?"

"No, and I don't think Mrs. Cabot did either. Somebody's killing folks, though. Third time this week."

"Yeah?"

"Yeah. Two guys at the hotel and a hooker out here in Arco Viejo."

Bishop drew a sharp breath. "Named Alexandra something?"

"Alejandra. Here in New Mexico, we roll that j. But yeah, Alejandra Ramirez. You know her?"

"Heard the name in passing, is all. How'd she die?"

"Same as the two guys at the hotel. Bludgeoned with a *bulto*." Williams shook his head. "Seemed like such a nice woman, you know? From everything the neighbors say, she had these two boys—nasty little bastards—got 'em taken away from her when she took up a smack habit. The priest raised them." Williams scratched the back of his neck. "Now one of 'em's my boss."

* * *

Seamus Caine scratched Alice's head, thinking. The little King Charles spaniel licked his hand and then nudged Caine's stomach, begging for more. With his free hand, Caine reached for his phone, sorted through his directory, found the number he wanted, and hit *call*.

"Oui…oui…oui, oui, oui," Edouard Doucet said as Caine spoke, running through the update on the authentication of the Zuni San Gabriel. "Frankly, I am happy to hear that Pablo Estrella is dead, yes? That he will no longer be swindling churches out of their precious *santos* and *retablos*."

"It was Interpol, you'll recall, that requested this investigation. And my appraiser is accused of Estrella's murder. Is there nothing you can do, Edouard?"

"*Mais non*. Interpol has no charter to intercede in a local murder case."

Caine said nothing. Trust Doucet to work for an agency that wouldn't dirty its hands with something as common as murder, dealing instead in tidier crimes—drug trafficking and smugglers of various sorts. But then, Doucet had always struck him as starchy. Nothing like the wonderfully earthy Frenchmen he'd come to know in Marseilles.

"Really, *mon ami*," Doucet said. "Estrella was buying the *santos*, or stealing them, *non*? What can Interpol do? Tell every priest in all of Catholicism to beware of a dead man?"

Chapter Thirty-Six

The only car available in Vista Cielo's rental fleet that afternoon had been an '85 Yugo, for which Colón made no apologies, though he knew a man of Phillip Cabot's height and station in life expected something larger, something more luxurious. This car, a rat wagon classic, was nothing like the Escalade Cabot had rented in the previous days of his stay.

The Yugo had no air conditioning, and the floor had rusted away in two spots on the driver's side, revealing the roadway beneath his feet. Colón handed him the keys with a smirk, but did no paperwork—almost as though he was so keen to see Cabot leave that it was worth sacrificing the Yugo just to get the job done.

Leave the car at the airport, Colón had told him. Don't worry about anyone stealing it—most people are too proud to want such a *pedazo de mierda*. Still, the *pedazo de mierda* ran, after a fashion, though it backfired occasionally as Cabot made his way out of town and back to the Cruz County sheriff's office in Arco Viejo, retracing his route to the jail he'd left earlier that day.

He did not appreciate returning to a place he'd been so eager to leave, but he had no choice. He was—and he couldn't believe he was, but he was—going there voluntarily.

Two deputies in front of the station laughed when Cabot turned off the ignition and the car coughed to a stop.

"*Hola*," Cabot waved to the two as he got out. "*Dónde esta Señora* Cabot, *por favor?*"

"*Señora* Cabot?" one of the deputies said, shrugging and looking at the other. "We have no *Señora* Cabot here. No women at all. Are you sure of the name, *Señor*?"

"Yes, she is my wife."

"Aieee—the wife is in trouble," the second deputy giggled.

"Are you sure? No women at all?"

"*Señor*, if we had women here, wouldn't we know?"

"Should I ask inside? Maybe she came in before you went on duty."

"Ask inside if you like, but you will get the same answer. There are no women in the jail today. None at all. *Nada*."

Cabot checked inside, asking if Sheriff Feliz had brought a woman in for detention.

The deputy frowned over his glasses. "Sheriff Feliz brings a woman to our jail? A joke, *qué no*?"

People peering over the tops of their glasses had begun to annoy Cabot. Or maybe, he thought, the gesture was intended to annoy him. Well, no dice—he refused to be annoyed. "No, no joke."

There was no mystery in that answer—he heard again what Colón had told him: 'Many women have, ah, been cleared of their crimes in Ordierno Feliz's bed.' Feliz had undoubtedly taken Wynn to his place. Perhaps she had gone willingly, to clear herself, or to do what he had done so often—find pleasure in someone else's arms.

In either case, Cabot knew where he was going next as the Yugo chattered and burped off in the direction of the Albuquerque airport. As he drove, he became more familiar with his new attitude. It felt good to be rid of the anxiety, the hurt. He hoped it would last.

He had to start trusting Wynn. She was, he realized, his hero—smart, confident, able to take care of herself in the world. All he could hope to be was her able assistant. He could do that. He *would* do that.

She was either in Feliz's custody or she was scouting for stolen art with the FBI. If she was in Feliz's calaboose, Cabot could run that attorney, Calderón, over to work his magic. And if she was with the Fibbie, she had a bodyguard—with a gun. She had a phone that he was pretty sure still contained his number. Cabot knew he'd done enough damage. She was hurt

CHAPTER THIRTY-SIX

and disappointed in him. He knew that too. And she didn't need him around right now. But he hoped she would call tonight to let him know how things turned out.

Chapter Thirty-Seven

Father Angel Hernandez stood just inside the door of the workshop, inspecting the work of one of Ignacio Garza's apprentices. The *bulto* did not yet have a cavity carved into the bottom of it. Good enough to sell into the gift shop market, he thought, but far from being the quality his overseas buyers expected. The young *santero* who had done the work was not yet sufficiently capable to replace pieces they'd swindled from the churches, certainly not accomplished enough to replace Ignacio Garza. But to create work for tourists? What would tourists know of the difference?

This piece could go to a gift shop attached to one of the restored Mission churches in the west, San Xavier del Bac, or San Luis Rey. Somewhere far enough away from the markets on the east coast and beyond, where Los Sapos sent the *bultos* with storage space in the bottom. A very small amount of space with a very, very large payoff.

Eliu Colón watched the comings and goings in the hotel lobby as though he was a bystander in a dream. For his employees and his guests, he cared not a whit, and he knew that wasn't how a general manager of a hotel should feel about his guests and his employees. He cared only about the building, the pool and stables, and dining terrace—he was proud of those.

Had been proud. At one time. He still was, of course he was, but the hotel wasn't what it had been. Unless El Eché sent him enough to pay the back mortgage payments, it would all be gone.

Additionally, the hotel needed an infusion of money to re-carpet the halls, re-paint the rooms, and re-fit the baths. The bedspreads had holes in them,

CHAPTER THIRTY-SEVEN

the drapes were worn and water-stained, the wood dressers bore cigarette burns from all those years when guests were permitted to smoke in the rooms. El Eché had promised that infusion of money at the end of the year. In two months' time. If he could keep the bank from foreclosing. If everyone could manage to stay alive that long.

Perhaps he could save the hotel yet. The *bultos* in the gift shop had something to do with the murders, that was clear. Both the man murdered in the gift shop and Pablo Estrella had known much about the subject of *santos* and both were dead. But the whore out in Arco Viejo had died the same way—what was the connection? And the Cabot woman also knew a good deal about *santos*—was she next?

What seemed certain was that the wheels were coming off out in Arco Viejo. He had the feeling something was about to occur that would endanger his getting the money for the hotel, and he couldn't let that happen.

He headed for the bar.

Neron Diaz had guzzled only two Pacificos that afternoon when Colón slid onto the bar stool next to him.

"You—" Diaz began.

"El Eché has decided not to pick up your bar tab anymore," Colón told him. "And he says he needs you to get to work."

Diaz picked his phone up off the bar and dialed. The voice on the other end, warm and familiar, said only, "No."

"Colón says you do not pay for my bar tabs anymore."

"That's why I said, 'No.' I knew you would ask. You drink too much. Get back out to Arco Viejo. And bring Colón with you. He and I need to talk."

Just past the sign marking the Cruz County line, the gold Corvette headed down into the canyon. The closer they came to Arco Viejo, the more Eliu Colón dreaded arriving there. He had heard about Ignacio Garza's accident. That event had effectively shut down the workshop. The other *santeros* could rough out the *bultos*, but the finish that made the difference between folk art and fine art, between icon and parody, had been in Garza's hands. On this, the Day of the Dead, the mood in Arco Viejo would not be joyous.

Diaz watched for spiders and snakes as he drove. He was happy for Colón's company—the last time he'd driven the road, he'd been visited by the dead—the ghost of Pablo Estrella, and he couldn't get the image of his own head, bouncing along the dusty road, out of his...well, his head.

Chapter Thirty-Eight

State Road 309, the road into Arco Viejo, hadn't been repaved in a generation. The asphalt had rutted deep with the weight and number of the trucks and cars that came and went these days. Feliz preferred to ride in the center of the road, on the ridges right or left of the ruts, to keep the low-slung patrol car from bottoming out in some of the channels.

He glanced up, trying to catch a glimpse of Wynn Cabot in the rearview mirror, seeing, instead, what looked like a Cruz County patrol car some distance behind him. He tensed, then shook it off. Villagers, he decided, coming home from selling their turquoise jewelry or silver work to the tourist fools that haunted the edges of Santa Fe plaza.

He looked again in the mirror and raised an eyebrow. Mrs. Cabot appeared to be sleeping. How could someone sleep on this rough road in this hot car? Did the woman not sense his palpable sexual charge now that they were alone?

He slammed on the brakes, throwing her forward into the metal mesh that divided the front seat from the back, separating captive from jailer.

"Sorry," he called as she pitched forward. "Prairie dog in the road. They make a terrible mess if you hit them."

They rode for another mile in silence before Feliz said, "How long had you known Estrella professionally before you...got to know him better?" Perhaps this had been his mistake. Perhaps he was rushing her.

"A few months."

Months? He wasn't going to wait months before he got to know Mrs. Cabot better. He had already waited days. He might wait a few more hours.

But months? Impossible. He had never waited that long for a woman.

And surely she knew more about Estrella than just his dealings with the *bultos*. "Did Señor Estrella ever talk about his life before you met? Where he went to school or...?"

Wynn thought. When they talked at all, they talked about the future more than the past—Pablo's ideas for what he would like to do in life, his family, where he would like to live. "No," she said. "I...no."

"Why were you and Señor Estrella no longer seeing each other?"

"Because I decided that my marriage was more valuable than what I had with... Señor Estrella." *There*, Wynn thought. *That should give him pause.* She'd understood Feliz's little pats, the stretch and pause at her hotel room door. She felt safe behind the mesh divider in the back of the patrol car—safer than she would have felt riding in the front seat.

Feliz sniffed. Of course, a woman would think a man like Phillip Cabot was valuable. He was very rich and a complete idiot. And apparently still in love with his wife. Feliz no longer had such illusions about marriage.

He glanced a third time in the rearview mirror. Cars behind him drew closer, a Cruz County patrol car, and behind that, a gold Corvette. He knew the Corvette's driver. A lifetime ago, the man had grown up beside him—a brother of sorts, before he became a Los Sapos soldier who had served time in the United States for running drugs. He knew the car's passenger as well—Eliu Colón.

Mrs. Cabot was lucky. If they hadn't been on such a well-traveled road, he would have stopped and given her a choice: submit to his desires or be left to the appetites of snakes and bobcats in the brush.

"So you left *Señor* Estrella?" Feliz asked.

"There was no leaving him—I lived in Houston. He lived somewhere else. I don't really know where—we always met at Vista Cielo."

"You had the ideal situation, *qué no?*"

"No, I wouldn't say so."

"Not ideal? A husband in Houston and a lover waiting for you here in our—" Feliz jerked the wheel to avoid a large tree trunk growing at the edge of the road.

CHAPTER THIRTY-EIGHT

Wynn braced herself with both hands against the back of the front seat. "I had left my husband before I met *Señor* Estrella." She fell silent for a moment, thinking. "Pablo did talk about his past one night. He admitted he had at one time worked for a company called Los Sapos."

Feliz nodded. "The Sapos are the U.S. arm of one of the bigger drug cartels in Mexico."

"He worked for them until his father was killed by a rival gang," Wynn continued. "After Pablo buried him, he tried to get out of the business."

Feliz remembered the incident, a drive-by shooting at a wedding a few years after he joined the police force. Not long afterward, Los Sapos had recruited Feliz to work from within to keep them informed of law enforcement's moves against their gang.

Funny, though, when he and Estrella muled for Los Sapos, between his last stint as sheriff and this one, Estrella hadn't mentioned his father's death. Now that he thought about it, Estrella hadn't talked about himself at all. He'd talked baseball or women or movies, but nothing personal ever came up.

"While he cast about for something else to do," Wynn continued, "he cooked up a scheme that provided smaller Catholic churches with the money they needed for their missionary projects by buying *bultos* and *retablos* and so forth out of the churches. The local parish priests really had no choice—they needed the money, as you might imagine. But he paid them so little that it amounted to a swindle. He thought he was being clever. I thought the idea was outrageous, and I told him so."

Wynn bit her lip, remembering the conversation that night. "He seemed astonished that I abhorred his scam. It was the only way, he claimed—otherwise, these beautiful treasures would never be appreciated by the audience they deserved. I disagreed. I thought they were not meant to be appreciated by a wider audience."

"But you deal in art objects such as this. How would you come to have met your *amante* if—"

"How indeed," Wynn said, watching the high desert spread out both right and left of the car while she remembered: Pablo, too, had argued that they never would have met had it not been for his idea to bring the *bultos* out of

153

the New Mexican villages to Caine et Cie in Houston. But his argument rang hollow with her, nothing more than a defense of his fraud.

"I told him the *santos* served their best purpose right where they were—to inspire the people who worshipped the saints they represented. We fought. I couldn't forgive his cheating the churches, and I left." She pressed her lips together tightly, fighting tears again. "I never saw him again…alive."

That last bit was a lie, she knew—she had seen him at the stables only two days ago, but Feliz seemed not to know of that, and telling him would only complicate an already difficult situation.

The outskirts of Arco Viejo were remarkably unremarkable—a clutch of mobile homes that telegraphed weary lives, and farther in, a commercial strip of a hardware store, a general store, a small grocery store, and a bar that rose from the middle of short scrub like a false-front western town.

What was eerie about Arco Viejo was that the streets sat empty, as though three hundred years after the Conquistadors left, the town had frozen in time—no electrical hoodoo, no people. Plastic skulls and skeletons blew in the breeze amid multi-colored crepe-paper streamers.

Feliz slowed the patrol car as he drove past the Cruz County sheriff's office, but he did not stop.

Wynn followed his gaze, seeing two deputies sitting out in front of the building, their wood chairs tipped back against the adobe. "Your office?"

"Yes. And my men. Loafing on the job."

"They're the first people we've seen since we got here."

"It's late. Siesta. No one will be out."

Wynn leaned forward and spoke through the metal mesh. "Down the road on your left," she said.

"I know, Mrs. Cabot. I grew up here."

She sat back. "Oh. I wasn't aware."

The cruiser rolled down the gravel street she and Bishop had traveled when they first came to Arco Viejo, and stopped in front of Ignacio Garza's workshop. Feliz revved the engine before he turned off the key.

"Now we will find out what is going on," he said to her and got out.

Chapter Thirty-Nine

Wynn stood just as Nerón Diaz nosed his gold Corvette in behind the police cruiser. Colón got out of the car, stretched like a cat in the warm afternoon sun, and looked around the square. He blotted his forehead with a Vista Cielo cocktail napkin.

Villagers watched from nearby.

"I'll be in the church," Colón said. "It'll be quieter."

Diaz suspected this whole mess had something to do with El Eché. Whatever it was, Diaz needed to keep the damage to a minimum. He withdrew his shotgun from the back of the car, held it up, and cocked it, the 'chick-chick' of the lever barely audible above a background grumble of tree frogs.

The cottonwood bonfire, set ablaze the night before to celebrate Halloween, still burned in the center of the square, radiating heat into an unseasonably-warm November afternoon. Three of the *santeros* tended the blaze.

"Stay there," Feliz mumbled to Wynn. Turning, he gasped at the passengers getting out of the police cruiser that had pulled in behind the Corvette. He unsnapped the strap on his holster as he approached Bishop and Williams. "Well, well. Agent Bishop. You turn up in the oddest places."

"Lotta people turning up in odd places," Williams murmured.

"Get out of here, both of you—I have a murder investigation to clean up here, and you're in the way. Williams, get back to the shop."

"Suit yourself, boss." Williams smiled. "If you need help, give a holler." He turned and winked at Bishop, ambled back toward the police cruiser, and struggled into the driver's seat. The forty pounds of attachments around his mid-section—radio, baton, cuffs, service pistol and ammo, taser, flashlight, and so much more—made fitting behind the wheel of the car tricky. But he wasn't going far; he knew better than to leave.

Feliz turned to Bishop. "And you, *Special Agent* Bishop, why don't you take your fancy-ass art-crimes investigation out of my county, and don't come back. If I find you anywhere near Cruz County in five minutes, I'll find you in violation of something that has a life sentence with no possibility of parole."

Bishop remained standing in front of Feliz. "I'm out here for several reasons, Feliz. First, Mrs. Cabot is my charge, not yours. Second, you stole my car—I intend to hold Cruz County accountable for that, by the way—and so I have no way of getting my fancy ass out of your county. And third, I have an investigation of my own in progress. Step aside." Bishop nudged Feliz with a hand and joined Wynn. "You okay?"

She nodded. "Where've you been?"

"Tied up."

From behind the metal-flake gold Corvette, a shotgun blast rang out. Heads turned from every corner of the plaza to see Nerón Diaz, a bottle of tequila in one hand and his shotgun in the other. He drank a slug, threw the bottle toward the bonfire, and shot at it, missing his target.

Feliz strode over to the skinhead, grabbed him by the back of his t-shirt, and hauled him away from the fire. "Are you stumbling drunk all the time, or just when you're doing business for El Eché?"

Diaz did not answer.

Gently, as though taking a toy from a child, Feliz took the shotgun from Diaz and rested it against an adobe wall about five feet away, too far for Diaz to reach it in one stride. Feliz put his arm around the skinhead's neck and pulled him close. "Why do you have to get shit-faced to do a simple task? Is life so bad?"

Life was not only bad, Diaz thought, but it seemed headed in the direction of worse. Whatever was going on here had attracted a crowd. Crowds weren't good for Los Sapos business. Five people nosing around and each of them for different reasons: Feliz and that deputy that shadowed him looking

CHAPTER THIRTY-NINE

for a killer; the redheaded woman trying to get out of a murder rap; Eliu Colón wanting to kiss El Eché's ass; and a guy he didn't recognize, but who dressed like some city gringo, probably here to oust Los Sapos from Cruz County.

He slumped. "Ignacio Garza hurt himself, and none of the others can carve so good," he whimpered. He tried to calculate how quickly he could get to the shotgun if he twisted free of Feliz's grasp.

"You need to close up shop here," Feliz said.

Diaz smirked. "Fine with me. These people don't do anything you tell them to do. Besides, they do not respect me. They do things to my car."

"But why go around killing people? Why do you attract this kind of attention to El Eché?"

Diaz glowered. "You had your killer, and you let him go. *Idiota*! That woman could not kill the way those men were killed—that takes a man." He thumped his chest with a thumb. "A man. You do not call me a killer when I am not. I am El Eché's second. No one talks to El Eché without talking to me first." Diaz pumped a fist in the air. "You disrespect El Eché, and you will be the one to die." He lunged for his shotgun, but Feliz took one step sideways and cut him off.

"You have met El Eché?"

"No one has ever met El Eché."

"But this is why you killed those men, because they disrespected the *jefé*?" Feliz asked.

"I did not kill those men. But I did you a favor. That whore needed killing. I went out there to rob her—the gringo Texan had just left, and I knew she'd have a bunch of money. She got all like, 'Oh, please don't shoot me—I'm your mom.' She pleaded. Said we was her sons—you and me."

"That's bullshit, Diaz."

"That's what I told her. She said oh, yeah, we was and she could prove it—just ask Father Hernandez."

Feliz frowned. Could that be right? Was that why she had given him money for his campaign—not to keep herself out of jail but because he was her son, and she wanted to see him succeed? Had she derided Lisa Guzman because

157

she wanted better for her boy, not because she was plying her trade? Was she doing things a mother would do?

In a single motion Feliz withdrew his pistol and fired a bullet at point-blank range into Diaz's heart.

Diaz crumpled.

Feliz fought a gag reflex at the smell of blood. He glanced at the blood spatter on his jacket and pants—damn. Damn, damn, damn. He'd paid good money for that jacket. His fury rose again to his temples, and he turned the gun on Wynn Cabot.

She held her hands out in front of her, as if to stop a bullet. "No!"

Feliz clenched his teeth. "Get into the church."

Turning, she found her feet and ran across the plaza.

Chapter Forty

Day of the Dead

Father Angel Hernandez had inherited Arco Viejo from his priestly predecessor forty years before. He'd tried to solve most of Arco Viejo's problems, and thought he'd made steps in that direction. His actions had not always had the desired effect—the parish remained poor despite his best efforts, the parishioners sinned more than they repented—but he had not left, and kept trying to please both his church and his earthly masters. Then he had made a discovery that lifted his town from poverty. Paid for good teachers. Clothed and fed his flock. Kept them occupied and out of mischief. Nine years ago, long after Ordierno Feliz and Nerón Diaz, the boys he had raised from small children, had left home—Feliz to study criminology in Albuquerque, Diaz to a life less noble in Mexico—he felt lonely without the noise of the boys around.

His parish took up so little of his time that he wandered the high desert aimlessly, sometimes not returning for a week, climbing into the mesas east of Arco Viejo. One mid-July afternoon, while he'd walked, a storm blew up, and Hernandez took shelter on the leeward side of a small butte, not far off from town. From his protected dugout and through the scrim of rain, he stared at a rock formation in the distance—what looked to him like a square, dark opening. When the rain abated, he walked across the dusty prairie, rolling his pant legs up from the mud, and pushed forward to investigate what he thought he'd seen—an almost-vertical mine shaft. Surely, he'd thought at the time, this was the dross of a silver mine, and so he had ignored it. Silver was plentiful in Father Hernandez's life, and cheap.

In a month, though, the lure of the mine shaft drew him back, and, equipped with ropes, flares, and water, Angel Hernandez began to explore what he subsequently named The Hernando. The mine lay on Santa Clara Indian land, he knew, and so whatever he found would belong to the tribe. But he had not expected to find something that changed his life, enriched his church, and taught him more about himself and the rest of mankind than he had ever expected to learn in a small, isolated New Mexico town.

Hernandez had discovered that he himself could be greedy, covetous, ambitious. And he found that he could kill. Twice he'd killed protecting The Hernando—once by strangling a hippie with a rope, a second time when he found a Santa Clara Native man poaching his stones, and he slashed the man's throat. The FBI and the local tribal police had searched for a while for the man from the pueblo; no one had come looking for the hippie.

He hid The Hernando cleverly while authorities nosed around, and he waited for almost a year before he began to work the mine for what he'd found there—not silver, but gold. And with the money he garnered from selling the ore he began to collect *bultos* of a quality beyond his dreams.

But he had ceded the town to Los Sapos. It was, after all, his fault that the cartel had come to Arco Viejo in the first place. He had brought this life—and sometimes death at the hands of the cartel—upon his parish, and he felt more than his usual burden of Catholic guilt for having done that.

Los Sapos had heard about Father Hernandez's mine through naïve villagers' loose lips and moved in to take over Arco Viejo. The cartels had increasingly turned to mining to raise cash and Los Sapos, tired of dealing drugs in a drug-hostile world, had jumped on the gold-mining bandwagon. Rather than lose The Hernando altogether, the priest became a complicit partner. He began to sell his revered *bultos*, with cavities cut into the bottoms of them, to far-flung markets, moving millions of dollars in gold to legal supply chains throughout the world. Los Sapos took their cut, and El Eché got his, leaving the priest with enough money to continue to collect *bultos*, if he lived modestly. Though he worked mightily to suppress the cardinal

CHAPTER FORTY

sin of wrath, he could not help but feel anger—Los Sapos had robbed him of The Lord's gracious gift of wealth.

The town had become Los Sapos's remote outpost in America's high desert—a base from which they could move within the U.S. without having to worry about people and goods crossing the border. In order for Arco Viejo to be the cartel's town, the townspeople had to be kept at bay. And only Father Angel Hernandez could keep them from going to the law.

Hernandez shook his head. To think… it had all begun because he had been lonely.

The law in Cruz County was Sheriff Ordierno Feliz. He had raised Feliz—where had he gone wrong? Or was there such a thing as evil that could not be driven out by good?

On this *Dios de los Muertos* the town celebrated many who had died this year, both the elderly and the few who had not escaped Arco Viejo but died trying. Arco Viejo itself was dying.

Father Hernandez stood in the church sacristy, robing for the ceremony that led the rites of the Day of the Dead—collar, shirt, pants, cassock, stole, alb, chasuble. He sighed, flipped the safety off his Beretta, slid it through a side slit in his cassock, and into his pants pocket.

He stepped into the sanctuary—the church's candles flickering against vagrant shadows, the altar bright with two of Ignacio Garza's most recent *retablos*: a gold-leaf covered Our Lady of Guadalupe on the left and a remarkable Saint Joseph to the right.

He stood reverently before the altar, listening to parishioners sing their doleful chants. And then the rattling of chains and muffled blows began, the occasional shriek and a groan—the sounds of the *penitentés* flogging themselves across their backs with whips of yucca strands.

Solemnly and one at a time, Hernandez began putting out the candles that lit the front of the altar, bowing as he extinguished each, murmuring a name and saying a prayer. Seven *penitentés*, wearing their familiar hoods, assembled at the back of the nave, waiting for the procession to the cemetery.

A flute wailed.

Hernandez smiled to himself as his heart swelled, hearing the sounds of the old believers. It was for these people, and indeed he was one of them, that he kept the timeworn ways.

When he was ordained he had, of course, imagined, in a sin of pride, that he might serve God as something more than a small-town parish priest in rural New Mexico. After repenting that worldly thought, he'd tried to live a righteous life, taking in Feliz and Diaz and trying to teach them the joy of living in piety. God had rewarded him not with a seat in the basilica but with a gold mine.

El Eché had demanded that more than half-a-million dollars worth of gold—perhaps the last batch of gold to ever come out of The Hernando mine—must be moved before the passes around Arco Viejo became impassible with the winter weather, when getting shipments out would be impossible.

Hernandez knew he must fearlessly follow God's word, but he was confused—was it God or Los Sapos who had, today, put a gun in his hand?

The villagers had gathered in the tiny church by the time the priest began to sing *Dios Nunca Muere,* Only God Never Dies.

The pale aqua walls of the church contrasted with massive dark beams on either side of the nave. Long hand-hewn benches and some homemade chairs provided seating for the worshippers. The altar—little more than a wooden table covered with a small black cloth—was decorated with tiny twinkling Christmas tree lights and garlands of paper skulls.

Garza sighed. One of his finest works, the crucifix, the most sacred, had been taken by Los Sapos when they first arrived. Many of his other fine pieces, too—works he had made out of devotion, as offerings, as gifts to his God—had disappeared over the years the bad men had occupied Arco Viejo.

So he prayed, as did they all, for deliverance from their slavery and victory over their captors. "*Dios mio,*" he began.

Wynn stood for a moment, waiting for her eyes to adjust to the dim interior of the church, then stepped forward, feeling as though she stood at the bottom of a deep pool. The aqua walls, with their flickering shadows, were the color

CHAPTER FORTY

of countless pools she'd swum in. As she walked to the front of the church, her feet and legs dragged heavily, much like the way she felt when she was in water well over her head. She gasped for air in the close heat of the church and the aftershock of seeing Diaz shot in the plaza.

The people sprinkled around the church sang a tune unfamiliar to her. Only a few of them even noticed her walking unsteadily forward to a bench. Her actions were intuitive, automatic: getting control of her breathing, she straightened and forced her diaphragm down, filled her lungs, and expelled the breath completely, then repeated the process until she didn't need to gasp. She paced the rhythms of each breath to her walk and to the singing of the people around her, breathing with them, feeling them.

Her mind gradually slowed. She gripped the edge of the bench and closed her eyes, forcing herself to think. What had Feliz done? Meted out renegade justice? It seemed rash, she thought, but he's a cop, and this is his county. She was fairly certain that Cruz County had due process, although Feliz might carry it out differently. Still, there would be courts and police procedure and investigations.

Except there didn't seem to be.

Like a rapid-fire slide show, images of Pablo's room flashed through Wynn's mind. Feliz had permitted the room to be cleaned immediately by the hotel staff—except for the blood on the grout in the tile floor—and neither he nor his men had ever made a move to search it. She herself had found the receipts. The Saint Joseph. The arm from another *santo*. If Feliz's people had been in there at all, they would have taken the items as evidence. Feliz had lied to her about that. He'd said he would conduct an investigation to prove—or disprove—Phillip's innocence.

But he hadn't, had he?

No. Feliz had taken Phillip to jail to show the public that the murders had been solved. And then he had jumped to the next conclusion—her own complicity—despite her protests to the contrary and the fact that all the evidence was circumstantial. He hadn't followed any procedure at all, but simply swaggered around in his Dolce & Gabbana jackets and his Donald J. Pliner shoes and took the easy way out, which included shooting a man who irritated him.

Wait.

Not the shooting…the clothes.

The slide show continued with pictures of Feliz. The jackets *were* Dolce & Gabbana, not cheap knockoffs; she'd seen enough of both at charity dinners and gallery openings, and she knew one thing: no one could fake those gilded logo buttons.

She ran the slide show in her head again.

Feliz's jacket was the real deal, as were the Pliner shoes and the Cartier watch. Not the tasteful black model but the gold one, showing out from under his sleeve for only a moment, then disappearing again when he flashed a monogrammed cuff.

She'd been such an idiot—he'd strutted it in her face, daring her to see it, but she hadn't. Feliz spent money—a lot of it—money that could hardly have come from a rural county sheriff's pay.

Maybe his family had money somewhere? Not likely. A genuinely wealthy man wouldn't wear designer clothes and flashy jewelry to a rank-and-file job. Only a boor would use those trappings to elevate himself above his real station. His fellow officers must resent him for that, she thought.

In her experience, a truly wealthy man—of any nationality—would not have boasted of his acquisitions. He wouldn't have to. What was it Feliz said? He'd bought a Fernando Botero from Phantom Gallery in Houston. She hadn't really believed it at the time, but now, as she thought about it closely, it made no sense at all. Though well-respected, Phantom put the edge in cutting edge, specializing in installations and video art, art with a modern social message. Angry artists with burlap clothing and egg-beater hair nailed their manifestos to Phantom's converted-warehouse walls and—

Except.

Except Feliz hadn't said he bought the Botero at Phantom, he'd bought it at Hampton. *Damn the fucking dyslexia again.*

Feliz said he was wined and dined by the gallery owner, and at the end of the evening, he bought a Botero from their gallery—Hampton Gallery.

Wynn almost laughed. Oh ho, Hampton was quite a different story indeed.

CHAPTER FORTY

Started by the Meadows brothers, Roberto and Benito, Hampton had been busted by a Houston TV station when a reporter noticed that the works Hampton sold were "remarkably similar" to legitimate works by local artists. Bobby and Benny Meadows, of course, denied any wrongdoing and had, since then, lowered Hampton's profile and claimed to sell only recognized masterworks.

Wynn grunted. Recognized. Recognized as fakes, that is. All the museums and art houses knew. But individual buyers—like Feliz—could still be swindled.

The slide show in her head faded to one last picture: Sheriff Feliz, the top law enforcement officer in a small county in a poor state, spent a lot of money propping up his lifestyle and dared the world to catch him.

Down the hill, Ordierno Feliz loosened his tie and set his fists on his hips as he watched *santeros* load cottonwood logs onto the trucks. Two others disassembled the saws.

He would move the operation north, closer to Ghost Ranch and its naive seekers of spiritual awakening. He would have to run for sheriff in Rio Arriba County but leaving Cruz County was just as well. There had been too many complaints that he was quick with a taser, that he never used his car camera, that he asked too much in bribes.

And, of course, any distance he could put between himself and Lisa Guzman might help loosen her grip on him.

He would be better able to control the way the drudges moved the *bultos* in and out of the state. And his operation would be closer to a major highway—no more driving these crappy roads. Shipping would be easier, as would commuting to Santa Fe and Albuquerque for his creature comforts.

"Hey, when you're done—" he yelled out to the men loading the truck. They did not look around when he spoke to them. He walked over to a man nearly as short as he, and tapped him on the shoulder. "Listen to me."

The man turned idly, studying Feliz as he chewed on a wad of tobacco, then leaned over and aimed a brown wad of spittle on the ground at Feliz's feet.

La audicia. The nerve. After they were finished loading the truck and the few other duties he had for them, this one would be next to die. "When you are through with the wood, take Garza and the woman from the church. Tie their hands and load them on the truck."

"*Pulga de perro,*" the man mumbled in Feliz's direction. Dog flea.

"*Prudenté*, Manuelito," the other *santero* whispered. Be careful.

"*Si, Manuelito,*" Feliz sneered. "*Prudenté*. When you have your *compadré* and the woman on the truck, take them out to the mine shaft and throw them in."

Manny shook his head matter-of-factly. "No. No, I won't. No one in this village could kill Ignacio Garza. His soul would return from the grave to haunt us for the rest of our lives."

"I'm telling you—you *will* do this."

"No, *señor*. That old *santero* is the last of his line. You want me to kill such a great and holy man—a man who is almost a saint? You can kill me first."

Feliz's index finger twitched at the thought. This insolent nobody would see his God soon enough, but Feliz needed him for a while yet.

He would get Garza and the woman from the church himself.

Feliz stood just inside the door of the church, waiting for the parishioners to finish their song, wishing he was in his air-conditioned patrol car on the way back to Vista Cielo for dinner, longing for the bitter splash of a Pacifico at the back of this throat. He squinted into the dark church, looking for Ignacio Garza but not seeing him in the crowd.

...Con la luz que agoniza
Pues la vida en su prisa
Nos conduce a morir...

He knew the song from his childhood—*Dios Nunca Muere*— a song that seemed to have a million verses. And what a racket—none of these people could carry a tune in a tub. Growing impatient for the song to end, he pulled out his pistol and fired a shot into the floorboards.

The villagers paused in their singing. A few looked over their shoulders, others shivered in fear. The priest raised his arms and began to sing once more,

CHAPTER FORTY

...Pero no importa saber
Que voy a tener el mismo final...

"Ignacio Garza," Feliz called out.

The priest stopped once more, but the old *santero* did not step forward.

Without dipping his fingers into the holy water font, Feliz walked up the center aisle, his gun hanging loose in his right hand. To his left, he spotted Eliu Colón sitting with his mother and old aunt, and then he saw Wynn Cabot near the front, on a bench near the confessional.

He strode up the aisle, stopped in front of her, and pulled her to her feet. "*Señora* Cabot, you will come with me."

Colón's throat tightened with emotion. He didn't care so much about what happened to Mrs. Cabot, but he suspected he knew what was going on—had maybe always known it—and he had to stop Feliz. He slowly stood, crept quietly out of the pew, down the center aisle and up behind the sheriff. As he leaned in, stretching for Feliz's gun, he heard a rattle and froze. He didn't know the sound, but he had always known that the sound would come, and that it would be otherworldly, and that he would hear it on this day when his father visited—the unmistakable clatter of bones bucking across the floor.

Some of the villagers heard the sound too. Others did not. As Colón expected: some had seen the truth of what his father had done to him when he was a child, and some had been blind to it even then.

He dared to look at the bones lying in a pile in front of the pulpit: a narrow skull with only five teeth, a rib cage, one hand, and three longer bones. The hand clutched a small whip. As he fell back, collapsing into the front pew, he called out, "Father Hernandez...did we not bury this man?"

The priest nodded his head. "He has crossed over, Eliu. Honor him and listen...."

The hand lifted from the pile of bones and pointed at Feliz. The jawbone chattered.

"No," Feliz pulled back. "It wasn't me—I saw you whip your son."

"Please, Daddy—go. Go back to the grave," Colón implored.

The skeletal hand moved to point at the priest. Villagers cried out: "You were wrong to whip the boy," and, "We know what happened, Eliu," and

167

"Your father is to blame."

Father Hernandez stepped forward and put an arm around Colón's shoulders. "Iguanito, your father had every right to do that. He made a mistake, of course. He hadn't meant to drown you—he was human. Human enough to realize his punishment had gone wrong. He's here to help."

"Don't call me Iguanito."

The priest ruffled Colón's hair paternally. "But it is part of who you are."

Colón pushed away from the priest. The money to revamp the hotel no longer mattered. He saw that. He faced the congregation. "I'm tired of the bullying and killing. No longer am I Iguanito, just as Ordierno Feliz is no longer El Eché. We must take that away from him."

Feliz snickered. "Me? I am not El Eché." He fired a single shot into the pile of bones.

Colón turned to Feliz. "Of course you are. Who else could El Eché be?"

A collective gasp went up in the church.

"I have killed no one."

"Sure you have," Wynn Cabot said. "Not half an hour ago."

The priest frowned. "Oh yes?"

"A man he called Diaz," Wynn said.

"Diaz." The priest sighed and cocked an eyebrow. So Nerón was dead. Well. A shame, and yet not surprising. "Your brother, Ordierno. You knew Nerón Diaz was your brother, *qué no?*"

"Shut up. We might have grown up here together but we—"

"You were Alejandra Ramirez's boys."

"That's a lie." Feliz fired a shot into the fresco of the Virgin behind the altar.

Parishioners cried out, "*Madré mio!*" and "*Cara Madré!*"

Feliz spoke through gritted teeth. "My mother went to El Paso."

"Your mother never got any farther than Española. She didn't want you to know what she did for a living, but she wanted to watch you grow up. She was, after all, a mother. And now, you've killed your brother. We should thank God she wasn't alive to see that."

"Diaz killed her. That's why I shot him."

CHAPTER FORTY

The priest took in a sharp breath.

"You killed the man in the gift shop, too, didn't you?" Wynn shouted out.

Colón nodded. "It had to be you, Ordierno. You were there too quickly after the murder."

Feliz grabbed Wynn Cabot's arm again and put the muzzle of his gun in her back. "Come with me." He lifted his voice so that it rang in the rafters. "Ignacio Garza, I will shoot Mrs. Cabot if you do not come forward, *comprende?*"

"*Por favor,*" the priest mumbled.

Feliz stopped, gaping at the priest's utter nerve interrupting him., He slowly tilted his head in the priest's direction. For the better part of his life, Father Hernandez had insisted that Feliz conduct himself like a gentleman, claiming manners would get him farther than bullying ever could. Feliz had the upper hand—a gun *and* a badge—and still, the priest dared to correct his manners? "Excuse me?"

The soft-spoken priest squared his shoulders. "I said, '*por favor,*' Ordierno. When you ask someone to do something, you should say, '*por favor.*'"

Feliz turned to Wynn and motioned. "*Señora* Cabot, you will come with me, *por favor.*"

The priest was beginning to irk Feliz beyond the headache that had already spread over the top of his skull, a dull throb brought on, no doubt, by the heat and the flies and the singing and the general catastrophe here in Arco Viejo. And he didn't appreciate Hernandez treating him like a child in front of these peasants. Apparently, the old priest did not want to believe what everyone had just heard from Colón, that he was El Eché. The head of Los Sapos. A man who murdered at first provocation, and whenever he could. A man never seen by anyone.

Father Hernandez sensed the fear that rippled through the congregation. He held his hands high in the air and then pressed them together. "Let us each say a special prayer…" He turned to the altar and bowed his head.

The church fell quiet, the living as silent as the slain.

Rather than pray, Hernandez knelt at the altar rail and thought. In that summer when Feliz was seventeen, and he rescued Eliu Colón from the quarry pond, Hernandez had thought the boy redeemed. But the world had embittered Ordierno Feliz's heart and so here, apparently, was the answer to his question—without repentance, good could not replace evil in Feliz's heart.

"Amen," Hernandez said and then rose and turned to face Feliz.

Feliz again scanned the parishioners. "Ignacio Garza, step forward…*por favor.*"

No one in the congregation moved.

"If you do not come forward, Garza…"

"…*por favor*," Father Hernandez prompted.

Still Garza did not appear.

Feliz's temples pounded. The dizzying headache had begun to nauseate him. He staggered a step and steadied himself on the pulpit. "Garza, I have already shot a man today," he yelled. "Shall I make it two?"

The confessional door creaked open, and Ignacio Garza stepped out. "I am here, making my last confession." He held up his bandaged hand. "The hand, it is infected. I fear it is the *tetano*. You would do me a favor if you shot me."

"Don't be stupid, Garza—you do not have the *tetano*. And I will not shoot you. You and the woman will come with me, that's all."

Obviously, Feliz thought, if he wanted this done, he would have to do it himself. These people did not have the courage to kill. He cuffed Garza's good arm to Wynn's right wrist, stuck his gun in the middle of her back, and pushed the two of them toward the front door of the church.

"*Por favor*," he said. "After you."

Chapter Forty-One

André Bishop ascended the hill from the workshop to the plaza. When he thought back on his visits to the arid southwest desert, he realized that his nose did better out here than in the humidity of Washington, D.C. He'd thought his condition had to do with D.C.'s smog in summer and the cold winds off the Potomac for the eternity that was each winter. His sinuses had cleared. He hadn't snuffled back a bloody nose in days. He could smell cottonwood smoke from the bonfire. With the exception of the bad situation he found himself in, he felt better than he had for years.

He felt better only until he saw Ordierno Feliz load Wynn and the *santero* into the back of his patrol car. *Damn it all*, Bishop thought. *Why am I always pulling up the rear flank? Really, I have to be better about my timing.* He ran into the plaza and stopped in front of the cruiser, wishing to hell he had a gun, a knife, a big stick. Something. Anything. "Feliz—stop right there."

Feliz stopped the cruiser for a moment, regarding Bishop casually as he lit a cigar. "Mrs. Cabot, your friend thinks he can stop a car by standing in front of it. Like Superman, *qué no*? Let us see if that works."

He dropped the car into low, gunned the engine, took his foot off the brake, and shot forward.

As he drove, he wondered how he had walked this road so many times as a teenager, and it had never seemed then, on foot, a long trip? The three-mile drive out to the quarry pond seemed to take twice as long by car as it ever took him to walk it. He jockeyed the patrol car around a pothole, the car's wheels bouncing off the sides of the deep cuts in the road.

Wynn leaned forward, speaking through the metal mesh that separated them. "Sheriff, listen to me. The villagers will know who is responsible if *Señor* Garza and I don't come back."

Feliz hit the brakes, put the car in neutral, and turned, glaring at his two passengers. "No, you listen to me, Mrs. Cabot. No one tells El Eché how to do his business. If you had any chance of living before, that has gone away. You have killed yourself and the *santero* with your foolish mouth. And I will not favor you with quick and painless deaths."

He put the car in gear and floored the accelerator. He would kill these two first and then go back to town and deal with Bishop and Colón. And there would be no bodies to dispose of out here. No, he knew a place that would take care of that for him—the quarry, at the sunlit entrance to a gold mine where, as a teenager, he'd grown his marijuana.

It was not El Eché who would do the killing. The quarry pond beckoned him back.

Feliz opened the back door of the cruiser and pulled Wynn Cabot from the car, Ignacio Garza stumbling out behind her. He walked the two, still handcuffed together, to the edge of the pond, chambered a round in his pistol, and pushed Garza in the middle of his back, firing a shot as the old *santero* dropped into the pond, yanking Wynn off her feet and in behind him, the handcuffs digging into her wrist. The shot ricocheted off the pond's stone edge and into the brush.

Garza hit the water flat—a belly flop if he'd been face down, but he was on his back—raising a splash just as Wynn smacked the surface face-first. Probably broke some blood vessels, she thought. The second she hit, she tucked her body. Then her arm, linked to Garza's, jerked upward with Garza's thrashing. She surfaced, tried to breathe. Garza's flailing yanked her half out of the water, then pulled her back in. It was clear Garza couldn't swim and that he was hysterical with fear.

"*Cueva de muerte!*" he yelled.

She had to do something; he was drowning. She could feel him "climbing

CHAPTER FORTY-ONE

the ladder"—vertical in the water, his arms and legs whipping up and down.

"*Calmar*," she called to him, evenly. She had to show him she could help. He stopped for a quick second, then lashed out again.

"*Calmar*," she said again, dodging a blow from his arm. She got her bearings, took a breath and circled.

Face down, she came up beneath him. Her back pushed against his, rolling him supine. Her arm, cuffed to his, stretched out, rigid. Scissor-kicking, she pushed him up, out of the water.

Garza's thrashing stopped. He eased for a moment. Wynn kicked savagely to keep the man afloat. But the effort took oxygen. She had to surface.

She rolled out from under him. He felt her support pull away, and he flailed again.

She took three deep breaths, dove, and rolled below him once more, pushing up. Garza calmed momentarily, and then began to struggle against her. She thought of violence. She could do it; she'd been trained to. Sometimes it was easier to clock a panicky victim than to fight on their behalf. But down here, they could be treading water for a long time. She needed Garza's cooperation.

Calling, "*Calmar*," she dove a third time, trying to heave Garza onto her back. The man fought to stay afloat, thrashing, screaming, pushing her farther under. He climbed onto her shoulders to get himself out of the water. Down they went, farther, sinking into the seemingly bottomless pond.

And then she felt it. Not the bottom, but an upward slope to one side of the pond. Which meant, if they followed it…

She pushed off from the bottom and surged upward. Now she was the one fighting. She clubbed at Garza's arms and legs until she caught his handcuffed arm. With a massive heave, she took his arm and hauled herself across his body. Then she wrapped her other arm around his neck. He jerked and rolled, but Wynn's grip on him held.

She kicked, kicked again, and a third time, each kick lifting Garza's head into the air. Three more kicks, and she felt the slope beneath her feet once more. She kicked twice more and then eased off. Touching down on the slope, she began to pull him up.

Garza panicked at first, but then he, too, felt the rocks beneath his feet—a slab large enough for them to lie on, a piece that had eroded from the hillside above and fallen into the hole. Lungs heaving, they scrambled for a finger hold and pulled themselves up onto the solid, slimy rock, their gasps punctuated with coughs and groans. Wynn leaned over and placed a finger on Garza's lips. "Ssh!"

He fell quiet, and the silence helped him understand. Better to play dead. "*Si*," he whispered.

All was quiet at the top of the quarry pond as well.

As soon as Feliz heard the two of them thrashing in the water, he had walked away. By the time the thrashing stopped, he was on his way back to Arco Viejo.

The *penitentés*, hoods up on their brown robes, moved out the door of the church in unison behind Father Hernandez and a small boy leading the procession bearing a newly hewn crucifix. Behind them, the rest of the congregation moved fitfully down the hill, some of them kneeling occasionally, praying and singing as they wound their way to the cemetery in the valley below the village.

André Bishop watched from a respectful distance.

At the cemetery, Father Hernandez stood among white-washed crucifixes and wooden grave markers and read out the prayers for the dead. And then, as dusk approached, the procession wound back toward the plaza in the same manner, stopping at the door of the *morada*—a long, windowless building adjacent to the church.

The old priest dropped back to the end of the procession and motioned André Bishop to join them. Bishop shook his head. "Go—tend to your flock. After tonight, you won't be saying Mass again. You know I have to arrest you, don't you?"

Hernandez chuckled and shook his head. "For what? What can you prove?"

Bishop sighed. This wasn't his turf, geographically or criminally, but he was the agent standing there. "Conspiracy, interstate transportation, forced labor. All the things you might expect. All the things that make what you

CHAPTER FORTY-ONE

were doing federal crimes."

From inside the *morada* came sounds of doleful singing.

"These people were not coerced. That is what makes the difference between my gold and the gold we read about, eh? The gold mined by people who are kidnapped to do the work? The conflict gold?"

"I think some of those folks might take exception to that, Father. We can probably find one or two of them who will testify."

Father Hernandez shrugged. "Suit yourself. You can try, but nothing will come of your investigation. Some of them became rich in my mine—stealing my gold—Los Sapos's gold. I do not think they would testify against Los Sapos."

The candlelight inside began to dim.

"I need to go in," Hernandez said. "The service will begin when all of the light has gone."

Bishop closed the door, the two of them on the outside. "We have a moment yet. What happened to the *bultos* when you shipped them out?"

Hernandez nodded. "Investors want gold without a history. When you have no history, you get a lower price for it, but it becomes much like the drugs the cartel had sold during the previous decades—people crave a bargain, *nó*? And Los Sapos had many investors. They bought our *bultos* as they would buy stock, and they bought in advance—ordering thirty, forty ounces to be…ah…to be included, shall we say, in the base of a *bulto*. Pablo Estrella was one of my best customers."

"You have any idea where Estrella's gold is?"

Hernandez shook his head. "By the way, I did not kill him. We fought, yes. And I hit him. I don't deny that. But he died when he hit his head on the edge of the pool. Check with the medical examiner. I did."

"And Sheriff Feliz—your own son—looked the other way while you moved the gold on to other markets."

Hernandez pulled open the door. "The service will begin."

Bishop stood aside. "I will be here when you come out."

Hernandez smiled. "I will not be coming out, Agent Bishop."

***

The peppery smell of piñon smoke from the smoldering bonfire perfumed the evening air. Cottonwood shadows fell long across the adobe buildings that surrounded the plaza. Tucked into the darkness, Bishop sat on a banco waiting, biding time, watching Feliz park the patrol car.

The sheriff opened the driver's side door, fidgeted with something on his dashboard, and then, as he began to get out of the car, Bishop bolted, rushing forward, slamming the door as hard as he could against Feliz's body. The point at the top corner of the door caught Feliz's left shoulder, and he howled.

Bishop pulled the door back and slammed it again, this time catching Feliz's right arm. The sheriff screamed in pain.

Bishop righted Feliz, pushed him back into the door opening, and threw all his weight against the door a third time, catching Feliz's windpipe between the door and the door frame. When he pulled the door open, Feliz crumpled, coughing, clutching his right arm, a dent visible halfway between his wrist and the elbow.

Bishop used his foot to roll Feliz onto his left side, pulled the sheriff's service pistol from its holster, and stepped back. "Get up."

Still on the ground, Feliz gagged.

"I said, on your feet, Feliz."

"You bastard," Feliz gasped. "My arm's broke. You'll do time for this."

"Nope. This time I have the law on my side, *comprende, amigo*?"

"I ain't your *amigo*."

"You're going to find out how few friends you have, I think. You leave the keys in the car?"

Feliz spat on Bishop's left shoe.

Bishop wiped the spittle on Feliz's sport coat and jerked the sheriff to his feet. He pulled a cable tie from the sheriff's jacket pocket and bound his hands behind him, Feliz moaning when Bishop moved his right arm into position.

"Now then. Let's try this again. You sold my car to a salvage yard, yes? So I'll need yours. And you took my gun, so I have yours. Oh, yes, I'll need a

CHAPTER FORTY-ONE

phone."

Bishop rummaged in the breast pocket of Feliz's sport coat until he found his cell phone. He turned it on, ran through the functions, and shrugged. "Ain't the latest, but it'll do." He reached over to the bonfire and pulled out a long cottonwood branch, still smoldering on one end. "Where did you take Mrs. Cabot and the *santero*?"

Feliz said nothing.

Bishop doubled the sheriff over the hood of the cruiser, pushing his face down against the metal. He singed the bottom edge of Feliz's sport coat with the smoldering branch. The fabric smoked and then caught fire. "That's good," Bishop said, still holding Feliz's head and shoulders against the car. "Gives new meaning to feeling the heat, eh?"

Santeros tending the fire hid their gleeful smiles—the sheriff was getting a dose of his own medicine.

Feliz twisted. "Put it out," he whimpered. "Put it out, Bishop. I took them to the quarry pond at the mine."

The smoldering blaze moved slowly up the back of the coat. Bishop figured he had another minute or so. "I wish you hadn't done that. You know, the minute you stuck this gun in my ass—*this gun right here*"—Bishop drilled Feliz's pistol into the sheriff's crotch—"you made this a Federal case. You knew that, right?"

"You're a motherfucker, Bishop. And you're too late. The Cabot woman and Garza are dead."

"Not if I know anything about the Cabot woman," Bishop said. He planted an elbow between Feliz's shoulder blades to hold him down, dropped the Beretta's clip, glanced at it, and slid it back into place. "Two shots left. Two shots left means I can miss once. And you know what?" He slapped at the embers on Feliz's jacket, extinguishing the glow. "I don't miss."

He opened the back door of the cruiser and shoved the sheriff inside. "All right, sheriff," he said. "Now it's your turn to ride in back."

Chapter Forty-Two

Wynn Cabot and Ignacio Garza lay gasping for several minutes in a dark corner of the quarry pond, water licking at the moss-slicked slab. As they rested, they sat up, quiet. Thinking. Shivering. The limestone radiated the promise of a November chill.

Garza glanced up. "Well, at least we have the moon tonight, *qué no?*"

Wynn looked up to see a gold moon rising over the rocky edge of the quarry. "Hunters' moon," she whispered.

"We can see the road back to town. And coyotes do not roam on the full moon."

She turned to him. "How's the hand?"

Garza nodded. "Cold water did it good." He chuckled. "Feliz might have done me a favor." He thought for a moment. "I am sorry I fought you. I don't swim."

Wynn sighed heavily, glad she had been able to save them both. "Are you all right? Can you walk?"

"I can walk, but do we walk, or should we wait until first light when we can see to climb out?"

Wynn pulled out her cell phone and knocked it against her hand, shaking out a small quantity of water, and then tried the screen. Nothing. She checked the sky. "We're losing daylight fast. Morning will be several hours away. How long will it take to walk back?"

Garza grabbed her arm. "Shhh. Listen."

The sound of tires on gravel came closer.

Garza sighed. "Feliz must be bringing someone else."

CHAPTER FORTY-TWO

Wynn grabbed Garza's good hand, and they climbed up the slab of limestone to a boulder near the top edge of the quarry.

Headlights swung around and paused at the edge of the pond, but did not extinguish. Then a car door opened and slammed. Footsteps crunched. Another car door opened. Voices growled, low. Feet scraped on gravel.

André Bishop pulled Feliz's cell phone from his pocket, along with the business card DaShaye Williams had given him and dialed the number on the back of the card. The phone rang four times on the other end before Williams picked up. He said nothing.

"It's Bishop. I got Feliz's phone—did I scare you?" Bishop chuckled. "Listen, Williams," "I'm calling with congratulations. You just won the election a few days early, buddy. You, my man, are the new sheriff in town."

Bishop listened to Williams for a moment, smiling. "Okay, here's what happened… Feliz shot a guy called Diaz. Nerón Diaz, yeah, I guess that's right. Plenty of witnesses. He admitted to killing the guy in the gift shop at the hotel, too. Actually, Diaz killed the prostitute, so that's off the table. And the priest admitted to killing Pablo Estrella. Well, he claims it was an accident…."

Bishop paused again and then, "I left Feliz out at the quarry pond. No, I didn't throw him in…Yeah, I probably should have, but professional ethics and all, you know? Gave him a wrap and a slap. You won't have any trouble finding him—he's hobbling around out there mad as a meat ax, so take backup."

Bishop, Wynn Cabot, and Ignacio Garza rode back to town in the patrol car, quiet and tired.

"Feliz looked a little pathetic, the way you left him," Wynn said.

"He won't go far. Williams will find him quick enough."

"I never would've thought to hitch one of his wrists to his ankles."

"Oh no? Like a calf in a roping contest? I'd have thought, you being from Houston, that you'd be familiar with two wraps and a hooey."

Wynn giggled. "Two wraps and a hooey?"

"Yes. You've never been to a rodeo?"

"No, I haven't. Where'd you learn it?"

"Grew up rodeoing, over in Louisiana."

"Ah. Is that where your name comes from?"

"Kind of. Mama was French, her people settled in Baton Rouge. Daddy came over from England after Viet Nam. Worked his way up at Air Liquide." Bishop paused, remembering for a moment. "In ninety-two, I went to study architecture at the Sorbonne. By then, Daddy had been promoted to corporate headquarters in Houston, but Mama's family was still in Louisiana. They kept the interstate hot, running back and forth. One Sunday evening, on their way home from a wedding in Breaux Bridge, both of them were killed in a freak accident."

"Oh, I'm so sorry. How old were you when you lost them?"

"Twenty." He snuffled and shook his head. "Just think—you and I might've met a long time ago if I'd stayed in Texas."

"Yes, well, we all take different turns."

Garza leaned forward from the back seat. "*Señor* Bishop, did you find out what was happening to our town? To our people?"

"You mean… about Father Hernandez and the gold? Yes, Ignacio, yes, I did. I talked to him earlier."

Wynn frowned. "Gold? What…?"

"Seems like one day some years ago, Father Hernandez was wandering the desert like an Israelite and stumbled on an abandoned gold mine. He decided to make the most of it so he and some of the villagers began to work that mine. He knew the villagers stole some of the ore, but there was enough to go around, and Hernandez didn't mind. Everybody was happy as a boy at a ball game."

"We took the ore to Denver or Albuquerque, or even to Mexico to sell," Garza said.

Bishop snorted to clear his nose. "And that was where the good people of Arco Viejo made their mistake. One day, Los Sapos—the American arm of a Mexican cartel—rode into town. They'd heard about the mine, and they took over."

CHAPTER FORTY-TWO

Garza sighed. "Terrible. The greed of those people."

"The top dog in Los Sapos was a notorious bastard called El Eché," Bishop continued. "Nobody knew who he was—he called the shots, but he was like the Wizard of Oz—no one ever saw him. That's because he had another name—Ordierno Feliz. And he had a day job—he was the local sheriff. But since he worked nine to five, Feliz—or rather El Eché—hired a local boy to run his day-to-day operation, a little shit he'd grown up with. A skinhead named Nerón Diaz."

Garza crossed himself. *"Madré mio."*

"Los Sapos smuggled the gold out in the bottoms of *bultos* that Ignacio and his people carved. Sold the stuff to buyers in large metals markets like Hong Kong and London—the *bultos* were really packaging more than anything."

Wynn nodded. "So that's why I was finding small cavities in the bottoms of the things."

"Yep. The buyers would acquire one for…say, twenty-five thousand, remove as much as fifty thousand dollars' worth of gold from its base, resell the gold into legitimate markets, put the *bulto* on a shelf, and go out and spend their new-found wealth on watches and champagne. Everybody got rich."

"Everybody but the *santeros*," Garza grumbled.

"Yep, everybody except the man at the bottom, Garza. Just like always."

"Still, we thank you for saving our town, *Señor* Bishop. If we'd had to fight, we wouldn't have done very well."

Bishop pulled the patrol car into the plaza, cut the headlights, and gasped. In front of him, half a dozen skeletons danced around the bonfire.

Ordierno Feliz hobbled along the rutted gravel road, hoping the skin walkers had not chosen the Day of the Dead to hunt. But of course, they would. What better night to go out than during a full-moon celebration? He sniffed the air for the tell-tale scent of rotting flesh that signaled the presence of the wolf-like creatures. His right arm had gone numb from the elbow down, the fingers of that hand had turned white.

He tried to summon his anger to help him break the plastic cable ties that bound his left wrist between his ankles. He gave a mighty tug, an effort that toppled him into the spikes of a yucca. The tie-wraps held.

Feliz caught sight of headlights, dim at first and then brighter and then brighter. A car stopped just in front of him, its headlights blinding him so that he could not see who it was that opened the car door.

DaShaye Williams shot a Q-beam in Feliz's direction. "You are a sorry sight," he called out.

Relief flooded through Feliz. "Williams—get me out of this mess. We have work to do in town."

"Well, I got work to do out here first." Williams pushed Feliz upright and chuckled at the sight: the little sheriff hunkered over like a mud turtle, his right arm dangling loose and broken.

Feliz was tired of being manhandled—first by Bishop and now by his own deputy. "Cut these ties," he said. "I have to get back. The FBI is going to find themselves minus one of their agents before this night is out."

"I don't guess they are, Feliz." Williams leaned down to look the sheriff in the face. "See, I'm here to arrest you for taking down Nerón Diaz."

"That was self-defense. He was going for his shotgun."

"Naw, he wasn't really, was he? You want me to go all Miranda on you or do you remember the words?"

"Cut these goddamned cable ties, and I mean *now*."

A second patrol car pulled in behind Williams's. Two of the night deputies got out, drew their pistols, and trained them on Feliz.

Williams pulled a pocket knife from his belt, cut the tie-wraps from around Feliz's ankles, straightened him up, and pulled his arms behind him. Feliz let out a yelp. "Fucking Bishop broke my arm—closed the car door on it. I'll arrest him for assaulting an officer of the peace."

Williams chuckled. "Oh, me. Oh, me... oh, my. Hurt you, did he? Assault with a what? With a car door? Is that even illegal? After what you did to him, I think a broken arm is getting off easy. Kidnapping a Fed would get you way worse than what you'll get from the state. Let it go."

Feliz wrenched away from Williams's grasp, finding the fury he'd tried to summon earlier. "You turn me the fuck loose, and I mean pronto! You don't

CHAPTER FORTY-TWO

know who I am, do you?"

Williams shoved the Q-beam in Feliz's face, impressed by the anger he saw there. "I know well enough who you are, you little jackass. And that's all I need to know." He opened the back door of the cruiser. "Get in before I kick you in."

A moon shadow followed André Bishop into the rectory. Without turning on the lights, he stepped to the bookshelves, searching, unsure what he looked for, knowing he'd recognize it when he found it. He pulled out a pocket flashlight and ran it along the edges of the shelves until he spotted a portion of one shelf at eye level where the dust had been recently disturbed and took out the books in that section. He riffled the pages of a hymnal. Nothing. Checked a Bible next in the stack. No. Lifted a third book and read the title: *The Sinners' Guide*. Ah, he thought, and looked at the top of the book. A folded piece of paper rose up over the tops of the pages.

He took the book to the rectory's desk, turned on the lamp, withdrew the folded paper, and read the message Hernandez had left. When he'd finished, he put the letter in the breast pocket of his jacket, turned off the lamp, and sat for a moment in the dark.

In the plaza, the bonfire burned bright. Villagers, costumed as skeletons, many of them wearing sombreros laden with cascades of marigolds, danced and drank, buoyed by the news that Los Sapos' hold on their lives had been broken.

Ignacio Garza stood, a large box of *bultos* nearby. He held high a San Gabriel and called out over the crackle of the fire: "My brothers and sisters, we celebrate tonight our new lives as well as the lives of those who have passed. We begin again, you and I, and I ask each of you to throw one of these—my unholy images created not for good but for evil—into the fire. Come on—let's burn Los Sapos out of our memory."

Eliu Colón rushed forward, blocking the villagers who reached into the box. "No—stop—how do you know which of these is a fake and which is the real one? Ignacio Garza is such a fine *santero* we cannot possibly tell the difference between one master and the other."

They paused, looked down at the carvings they held, and then turned away from the fire.

Only Manny spoke. "But didn't Father Hernandez sell the real San Gabriel to a man who buys such things? And that man sold it to the museum in Santa Fe, *qué no?*"

"No, Manny," Colón said. "Father Hernandez conned a con. The *bulto* he sold to *Señor* Estrella was not Pacheco's—the San Gabriel that Estrella bought, and then sold to the Folk Art Museum was one of Garza's, but Estrella never knew it. You see? If you do not know the difference between a fake and the real thing, you will believe it to be real, yes?"

"So, do we still have Pacheco's San Gabriel?"

Garza stepped forward, chuckling. "Yes. Yes, we do. When Feliz gave it to me to duplicate, I did one copy as quickly—and as accurately—as I could. Perhaps that was the one Father Hernandez sold to Pablo Estrella, I don't know. I hid the Pacheco in the sawdust in our workshop." He smiled. "Who would think to look in a pile of sawdust?"

Shortly after he'd risen at his usual time of 4 AM, Seamus Caine's phone chimed, indicating a text message. He glanced at the caller ID and frowned, recognizing the area code—505—but not the number. The text read "Okay here, FBI to the rescue. Will call soon. Wynn." Caine nodded and sighed. Of course she was okay. He wouldn't have to call out the militia—that could be saved for another day.

Chapter Forty-Three

November 3

Wynn Cabot, André Bishop, and Ignacio Garza drove west on a narrow two-lane highway across the Navajo reservation toward the Zuni pueblo lands. The landscape flattened, mesas no longer obscured the horizon line. Dust devils swirled and gasped for air, the sun thin as a memory of summer.

The Zuni Pueblo Visitors' Center, a low oblong in the middle of a desolate parking lot, sat dark, its doors locked. The tourist season had ended a month before. The three of them peered into the building's windows, trying to make out what they could of the display of folk art: kachinas, pottery, *santos*. At the side of the display was a plexiglas case with a single piece—a *bulto* of Saint Michael, the companion piece to the Zuni San Gabriel.

"Help you?"

Bishop turned and pulled out his FBI ID. "Lusita? Lusita Begaye? I'm Agent Bishop, FBI."

The Zuni woman pulled a ring of keys from her pocket and unlocked the door of the welcome center. She stepped in, motioning for Bishop, Wynn, and Ignacio Garza to follow. "It's there," she indicated, pointing to the Saint Michael. "Want me to take the cover off?"

Wynn nodded. "Yes, please. This is Ignacio Garza, Ms. Begaye."

"The *santero*. An honor, sir." Lusita Begaye held out her right hand before she noticed Garza's hand, heavily bandaged. "Oh, sorry. Carving accident?"

Garza took her right hand in his left. "It'll heal. A couple of months, the doctors say. Could've been worse. By the grace of our Holy Father the nerves weren't cut."

"Good. We can't lose men like you, sir. Too few of you left. So. On to the Saint Michael, eh?"

Wynn Cabot slipped on white cotton gloves and turned the *bulto* on its stand. "May I hold it?"

Lusita Begaye lifted the *bulto* from its pedestal. "For a moment."

Wynn took it and held it to her nose, then closed her eyes and cradled it to her cheek. She smelled it once more and then held it out to Ignacio Garza so that he might see it.

Garza's eyes filled with tears, and he dropped to one knee, crossing himself.

They waited until he rose before anyone spoke.

Lusita Begaye sighed. "I'm sure you know its story, yes?"

They nodded.

Garza wiped his eyes with his shirt sleeve. "He was a true master, Pacheco. I shall never be holy enough to do this kind of work, but I will spend the rest of my life trying." He stroked the shield St. Michael held. "A true master."

Wynn frowned. "When the Smithsonian returned the piece to New Mexico, the church didn't ask for it?"

Lusita Begaye smiled. "Our governor made sure the church knew where it belonged."

Wynn replaced the Saint Michael on its stand, looked at André Bishop and nodded. "Our San Gabriel is from the same hands. Both of them carved in seventeen-seventy-five."

"I have brought you something," Garza said. He set a gym bag on the floor and unzipped it with his good left hand. Gently he withdrew and unwrapped the companion piece—the Zuni San Gabriel. "He has come home, to be with his brother."

Lusita Begaye bit her lower lip. "Blessed Saint Gabriel…" With trembling hands, she reached forward and took the *bulto* from Garza as though she rocked a baby.

"Take care of him," Bishop said. "Blood has spilled because he was not

CHAPTER FORTY-THREE

where he should be."

Lusita placed the Zuni San Gabriel on the same pedestal as the companion piece, covered both of them with the fiberglass casing, and locked it, but did not withdraw her hands from the case. She looked thoughtfully at the two carvings. "We Zunis have a blessing," she said. "This night our fathers, all the masked gods of the mountain and lake, assume human form to preserve what has been since the first beginning." She looked at Garza. "Thank you."

Chapter Forty-Four

Late November

At FBI headquarters in Washington D.C., André Bishop put down his newspaper, reached for his cell phone, and dialed Wynn Cabot's cell phone number. For weeks he'd been fishing for a reason to call her, and now he had two. "Bishop here," he said when she answered. "How was your trip home?" He smiled. "You renewed your lease? Good."

Well, it was good news and a disappointment both, he thought. She hadn't gone back to her husband, and that was a relief, but her lease renewal was a setback to one of his reasons for calling. Still, it wasn't insurmountable.

"You left before the real fun began—Father Hernandez's letter told us where to find him. Or rather, his body. Yes, I'm afraid so. He went out to his mine and ate the rest of his nitroglycerine. He left us the names of the other Los Sapos members, so we rounded them up and found them some beds in Supermax. I don't think Arco Viejo will see any of them again."

He listened to her voice, deep in her throat in that plummy Texas drawl. He watched a light snow begin to settle on Pennsylvania Avenue, snarling traffic once again as she asked about him—what was he working on? How had the surgery on his nose gone? He smiled. "I'm better, thanks," he said. "Back at the office. The surgery went fine. Still a little green and yellow around the eyes. No more nose problems, though, and that's a relief."

Neither of them spoke for a moment, and Bishop listened to the easy silence on the line.

CHAPTER FORTY-FOUR

"Listen," he said finally. "Do you remember that *bulto* of Garza's that sold at Sotheby's London auction? Bought by the Church of something something? Yes, that's it, Immaculate Heart of Mary. The piece that started it all. Well, I was just reading in *The Guardian*...yes, I do. I read *The Guardian*, okay? Listen to this: 'On Thursday night, 21 November, just when the Brompton Oratory in London began the celebration of its feast day, bringing out their holy relics, their recently-acquired icon of Saint Gabriel began to issue a stream of a watery or oily substance from the corner of its right eye, which eventually took the form of a long cross that covered the icon's body, and as the cross formed the figure began emitting a fragrance.'"

He tossed the newspaper on the desk. "Are we sure we gave the real San Gabriel back to the Zunis?"

He listened for a moment to her reasons for authenticating the *bulto*—the sense she had of its age, how the workmanship matched exactly to that of the Saint Michael at the Zuni pueblo's Visitors Center. They could date the wood in both pieces all they wanted, but yes, she was sure.

She *was* whip-smart—Caine had been right about that—and easy to talk to. All the time he'd worked with her in New Mexico, he hadn't worried once about not saying the right thing.

He took a deep breath and began the second of his reasons for the phone call. "Look... one of our Art Crimes agents has transferred to another division. We have an empty desk—a position for someone with your...ah...training. I know you just renewed your lease, but if you're interested, interviews begin just after the first of the year and—"

He heard a whoop and a "Hell, yes!" on the other end of the line.

He chuckled. "I guess that means I should arrange ..."

Epilogue

Now André had asked her to move halfway back across the country again, this time to New Orleans.

His request felt rushed, out of the blue somehow. She barely had her groove at the FBI yet. There was always one more forgery to expose, one more con to solve. She'd miss André, but if she stayed at the Bureau, dived in even deeper, the way she worked at her Olympic training—corrected her mistakes, made the good better, and put in the reps—she could help clean up the art world with the resources of the Bureau behind her.

Maximizing what he'd originally recruited her for.

What her dyslexia made her perfect for.

What she loved.

A Note from the Author

Mexican cartels, increasingly weary of dodging drug enforcement and tired of the layered structure of dealing drugs have, as recently as 2013, turned to gold mining as a revenue stream and a mechanism for laundering money. As much as nine percent of Mexico's multi-billion-dollar gold industry is a result of illegal production controlled by the cartels. Gangs demand extortion payments from locals and multinational mine operators in exchange for allowing them to work their concessions, or take full control over a mining operation.

Often citizens are kidnapped to work the mines to produce what is known as "conflict gold." It is the opinion of many policing agencies that the fourteen students kidnapped in 2014 were sent to far-flung gold mines as conscripts, never to be heard from again.

Carving *santos* is an enduring tradition from Central and South America, the American Southwest, the Caribbean, the Philippines, and Spain. Traditional *santos* take two forms: carved wooden sculptures called *bultos* and flat paintings on wood called *retablos*. The work of early *santeros* is still present in churches throughout Northern New Mexico, providing inspiration for the sacred art of today.

About the Author

Drew Golden is the award-winning writing team of sisters Cynthia Drew and Joan Golden. Asheville, North Carolina resident Cynthia Drew is the recipient of the 2017 INDIE Gold Award for Best Mystery and is a certified private investigator. Joan Golden is an Albuquerque, New Mexico resident and award-winning screenwriter.

Also by Drew Golden

Other books in the Wynn Cabot Mystery Series published by Level Best Books:
Nouveau Noir
Side Hustle

Numerous works by both authors outside of this series